I0653399

Francis Dennis Massy Dawson

# The Scripture doctrine of the Holy Eucharist

Francis Dennis Massy Dawson

**The Scripture doctrine of the Holy Eucharist**

ISBN/EAN: 9783742829337

Manufactured in Europe, USA, Canada, Australia, Japa

Cover: Foto ©Andreas Hilbeck / pixelio.de

Manufactured and distributed by brebook publishing software
(www.brebook.com)

Francis Dennis Massy Dawson

# The Scripture doctrine of the Holy Eucharist

# THE SCRIPTURE DOCTRINE

OF

# THE HOLY EUCHARIST.

BY

## FRANCIS DENNIS MASSY DAWSON,

OF THE MIDDLE TEMPLE, BARRISTER-AT-LAW.

AUTHOR OF "THOUGHTS ON THE MILLENNIUM AND FIRST RESURRECTION,"
AND OF "THE APOSTOLIC SUCCESSION AND ANGLICAN CHURCH."

LONDON:
JAMES NISBET & CO., 21 BERNERS STREET.
MDCCCLXX.

TO

MY SON,

## FRANCIS STAUNTON MASSY DAWSON,

THE FOLLOWING

### Treatise

IS

AFFECTIONATELY DEDICATED.

# PREFACE.

In the following attempted exposition of the Scripture doctrine of the Holy Eucharist, I have found it impossible to do justice to the subject without investigating the views entertained by Roman Catholics on the question of transubstantiation ; and, that I might.not be charged with misrepresenting their views, I have taken them from what I conceive to be the highest and most unexceptionable authority, namely, the second and revised edition of the fourteenth, fifteenth, and sixteenth lectures on " The Principal Doctrines and Practices of the Catholic Church," by the late Cardinal Wiseman. It did not fall within my scheme to notice the preliminary lectures, and, therefore, I have not troubled my reader with any observations upon them.

My references to the New Testament are to the edition of our authorised version lately edited by Tischendorf, and published by Tauchnitz. It contains a valuable introduction by the distinguished editor, and various readings from the three most celebrated manuscripts of the original Greek text,—the Sinaitic, the Vatican, and the Alexandrian, which are respectively referred to by the letters S., V., and A.

I have sometimes also had occasion to refer to the Peschito, but my knowledge of it is limited to the translations by the late Mr Etheridge. The Peschito* has always been held in the highest esteem by the Syrian Churches, and there is strong circumstantial evidence that it was compiled during the first century, before John had returned from his banishment to the Isle of Patmos. The better opinion seems to be, that, probably during the third and fourth centuries, the Syrian version was partially revised and reduced to its present form, to make it more in accordance with the Greek MSS. then current at Antioch, Edessa, or Nisibis; and Dr Tregelles thinks he can detect indications of even later changes. (See a learned dissertation on the

---

* This word is variously spelt by different authors. The late Mr Etheridge used to write it as above, but Dr Cureton spelt it without the c, thus—" Peshito " (see Nitrian Fragments); so also Dr Tregelles (see Smith's " Dictionary of the Bible," tit. " Versions "); and Dr Wright adopts the following form—" Pĕshĭttā " (see Preface to " Ancient Syriac Documents," edited by Dr Wright).

subject in Smith's "Dictionary of the Bible," *tit.* "Versions.") I myself have read the article several times in the hope of ascertaining the precise degree of estimation entertained of the Peschito by so competent an authority; but I confess I have not succeeded. The general impression it left upon my mind, when taken together with what others had written, was that, allowance being made for the modifications above alluded to, and which, it seems, are easily distinguishable to the eye of sufficiently skilled expert, the Peschito is, of all the versions we possess, with the exception of the Nitrian Fragments, the nearest approach to a correct translation of the Gospels' and Epistles, as originally written by the Evangelists and Apostles.

In his introduction to our authorised version, Tischendorf says, " I have no doubt that, in the very earliest ages after our Holy Scriptures were written, and before the Church protected them, wilful alterations, and especially additions, were made in them " (p. xv.) ; and the reader is doubtless aware that men of the highest order of intellect have devoted their lives and energies to the work of restoration. Hence, several spurious texts have been detected and many a genuine one restored to its original reading. On a cursory comparison of the results thus obtained with Mr Etheridge's translation of the Peschito, it appears to me, that in proportion as the learned are agreed upon any matter of amendment, almost in the same proportion do they approximate to the reading of the Peschito.

An argument had been urged by the late Dr Adam Clarke in favour of his interpretation of the form of institution, founded on the peculiarities of the Aramaic language, the soundness of which had been controverted by the late Cardinal Wiseman. The question in dispute between them appearing to me to involve matter of considerable interest, I submitted a case for the opinion of a learned Hebrew professor, and the reader will find the case and opinion in the Appendix.

I have to acknowledge my thanks to my esteemed friend, H. Howlett, Esq., for his valuable assistance in verifying the texts and correcting the press.

# PART THE FIRST.

---

"NOSCITUR A SOCIIS."

# CHAPTER I.

As the only persons who are interested in the result of the present inquiry are those who believe in the divine inspiration of the volume of the sacred law, however they may differ in respect to the nature and degree of such inspiration, I shall assume, as a fundamental hypothesis, that He who created the material universe is also, either directly or indirectly, substantially or plenarily, the Author of the Holy Scriptures.

In the Gospels we have three accounts of the institution of the Last Supper, viz., one by Matthew (xxvi. 26-29), another by Mark (xiv. 22-25), and a third by Luke (xxii. 14-20). There is also a fourth account by Paul (1 Cor. xi. 23-25), which he tells us he received directly from the Lord. John is silent on the subject, though he enters very fully into other matters, and gives a detailed report of the Lord's address to the apostles after the supper had ended.

But in the sixth chapter of the Gospel according to John, there are some remarkable words attributed to Christ, which, though they were not spoken on the occasion of the Last Supper, are often referred to as confirmatory of the Real Presence. In the course of a long address, at which there was a mixed company assembled, consisting of the apostles and general disciples, our Lord is reported, among other things, to have spoken as follows:—" Verily, verily, I say unto you, Except ye eat the flesh of the Son of man, and drink His blood, ye have no life in you. Whoso eateth my flesh, and drinketh my blood, hath eternal life; and I will raise him up at the last day " (John vi. 53, 54).

I am not aware that anything turns upon the rendering of the above text. On the contrary, our received version seems to be a sufficiently correct translation of the original into English; and, such being the case, it follows that, in some sense or other, we are expressly told to eat the flesh and to drink the blood of Christ. The only difficulty, therefore, is in ascertaining the sense in which we are to eat the one and to drink the other.

If the words are to be taken in their ordinary literal sense, then it would appear that we are directed to eat the natural flesh and to drink the natural blood of Christ. This is as obviously the case, as to our ordinary senses it is obviously the fact that the sun revolves round the earth during the course of every four-and-twenty hours. But as our experience in scientific inquiries teaches us how dangerous it is to generalise on isolated phenomena, so are we also cautioned against a similar practice in the interpretation of the Scriptures. For we are expressly told, " Judge not according to the appearance, but judge righteous judgment" (John vii. 24).

That there was some obscurity in the language of our Saviour, may be collected from the conduct of those who heard it. For whilst some of His disciples went back and walked no more with Him, others, who were probably more familiar with His sudden transitions from the natural to the spiritual, said, " This is an hard saying; who can hear it?" thereby implying that there might possibly be some mystery involved in His language which they could not understand.

In illustration of this peculiarity of the Lord's style of speech, the New Testament affords a variety of instances. Thus we read in John viii. 51, " Verily, verily, I say unto you, If a man keep my saying, he shall never see death." The original is, $\theta\epsilon\omega\rho\epsilon\hat{\iota}\nu$ $\theta\acute{a}\nu a\tau o\nu$, a Hebraism for *to die*. (See Alford and Parkhurst *in loc.*) Hence it would seem that those who kept the sayings of Christ would never undergo the ordinary process of dissolution; a sentiment, which, if possible, is even more emphatically ex-

pressed in the 25th and 26th verses of the eleventh of
John, where Jesus, speaking to Martha, says, " He
that believeth in me, though he were dead" (original
ἀποθάνῃ, in the past tense, *have died*, though he have
died), "yet shall he live ; and whosoever liveth" (original πᾶς ὁ ζῶν) "and believeth in me, shall never die."
Here, as Alford observes, "the word ζῶν must be
taken of physical life, for it stands opposed to ἀποθάνῃ.
Hence the inference from the grammatical construction of the sentence would be, that, inasmuch as
Christ, when He says, ' he that liveth,' is speaking of
physical life, so when He says, ' shall never die,' He
must also be understood as speaking of physical
death." (Alford, Gr. Test., *in loc.*) So that, construed
literally, nothing can be more apparently the case
than that our Saviour, in the most direct and explicit
terms, declared that those who believed in Him
should never experience physical death ; and such
was the meaning attached to His words by those who
heard Him (John viii. 52). But now that we are
enabled to interpret His words by the events that
have happened, we are sufficiently informed to know
that His apparent was not His real meaning, and
that, if we persistently refuse to recognise a spiritual
sense, the ordinary rules of grammatical criticism,
though affording an excellent test in respect to human
compositions, if rigidly applied to the interpretation of
the language of Christ, would often lead us into error.

There is another peculiarity of the Lord's mode of speaking which is of importance to a correct interpretation of His language. It is notoriously the fact that our Saviour often so expressed Himself that the apostles, as well as others who were present, were unable to comprehend His meaning. On such occasions, He would sometimes condescend to explain Himself; at other times, He left it to the progress of events to develop the purport of what He had said; and then, again, it not unfrequently happened that He would adopt a middle course, by which I mean that He would explain what He had said, but so that His explanation was as mystical and incomprehensible to His hearers as the text itself.

Many passages of our Saviour's ministry will suggest themselves in illustration of the first class of difficulties. I shall, therefore, only refer to one or two; such as when the lawyer asked Him, "Who is my neighbour?" (Luke x. 29). Similarly, when He was asked to explain the parable of the sower (Mark iv. 10–20).

In illustration of the second class, take the following instances:—

We are told that the people who were with Him, "were all amazed at the mighty power of God. But while they wondered every one at all things which Jesus did, He said unto His disciples, Let these sayings sink down into your ears: for the Son

of man shall be delivered into the hands of men."
And we are further told, " But they understood not
this saying, and it was hid from them, that they
perceived it not: and they feared to ask Him of that
saying" (Luke ix. 43 45). So also in the case of
the woman of Samaria at Jacob's Well, Christ having
told her that, " Whosoever drinketh of the water
that I shall give him, shall never thirst; but the
water that I shall give him shall be in him a well of
water springing up into everlasting life. The woman
saith unto Him, Sir, give me this water, that I thirst
not, neither come hither to draw." Thus evincing
her utter misconception of His meaning. Whereupon our Lord, instead of explaining Himself, turned
the conversation to an entirely different subject, and
" saith unto her, Go, call thy husband, and come
hither" (John iv. 14–16).

But the most remarkable illustration of the apparently studied obscurity in the language of the
Lord is what is narrated of Him by John, on the
occasion of His driving out the persons who were
merchandising in the temple. The Jews, who were
naturally surprised at what He had done, as well as at
the authoritative tone of His language, said unto Him,
" What sign showest thou unto us, seeing that
thou doest these things ? Jesus answered and said,
Destroy this temple, and in three days I will raise
it up" (John ii. 18, 19). There is no mention of

this incident in the other Gospels, but it is recorded by John, who was personally present on the occasion, and who, as Eusebius states in his "Ecclesiastical History," Book iii., chap. 24, was fully aware of what the other Evangelists had written. It is further of importance to note that no dispute or recorded variance exists as to the meaning of the actual words that our Lord made use of, and which are correctly rendered in our received translation: "Destroy this temple (λύσατε τὸν ναὸν τοῦτον) and in three days I will raise it up." What temple? Why, apparently the temple in the court of which (ἱερόν) He was then standing, and whence He had expelled the money-changers, viz., the temple of Jerusalem. And He was aware that He was so understood by those who heard Him. "Then, said the Jews, Forty and six years was this temple (ὁ ναὸς οὗτος) in building, and wilt thou rear it up in three days?" Hence our Saviour was aware that He was understood, by "*this temple*," to mean the temple of Jerusalem, and as He did not make any reply to the question the by-standers put to Him, the natural inference in their minds would be, that He assented to their interpretation.

Let us now turn to what occurred on the occasion of Christ being brought before Caiaphas, the high priest.

We read in Matthew as follows :—" Now the chief

priests, and elders, and all the council, sought false witness against Jesus, to put Him to death; but found none : yea, though many false witnesses came, yet found they none. At the last came two *false witnesses*, and said, This fellow * said, I am able to destroy the temple of God, and to build it in three days" (Matt. xxvi. 59–61). Mark gives a similar account of what took place. "And there arose certain and bare *false witness* against Him, saying, We heard Him say, I will destroy this temple that is made with hands, and within three days I will build another made without hands. But neither so did their witness agree together" (Mark xiv. 57–59).

It is to be observed that both Matthew and Mark agree in describing these witnesses, the one (Matt.) as false witnesses (ψευδομάρτυρες) ; the other (Mark) as bearing false witness (ἐψευδομαρτύρουν): and though John had explained the origin of the error, he leaves the imputation against the veracity of the witnesses as he found it.

Now, in what sense can it be predicated of these men that they were *false witnesses?* We learn from John what the precise words were that the Lord had used, and from what we read in Matthew and Mark, they were not accurately repeated by the witnesses. But that is almost invariably the case where

---

* In the original there is no word corresponding to *fellow*. But the form of expression (οὗτος) is indicative of disrespect.

several persons depose to what has fallen in the
course of a verbal communication. Witnesses of the
most unimpeachable veracity will often disagree as
to the precise words that were spoken.

All we look for on such occasions is the substantial
truth, not the *verbatim ;* and on the trial before
Caiaphas there is no substantial difference between
the evidence of the witnesses and the narration of
John. What the witnesses in substance said was,
that they had heard Christ declare that if the temple
of Jerusalem were destroyed, He could rebuild it in
three days ; and according to John, He was so understood to have said by those who were present. It
is further to be remarked, that the Lord does not
complain of any verbal inaccuracy ; for we read in
Matthew xxvi. 62, 63, " And the high priest arose,
and said unto Him, answerest thou nothing ? What
is it which these witness against thee ? But Jesus
held His peace."

Wherein, then, were these men *false witnesses ?*
I take the answer to be, that they were false witnesses in this : that by their evidence they intended
to convey that what our Lord said He spoke of the
temple composed of stone and mortar, whereas in
truth the temple was symbolic of Himself, and it
was only as a symbol of Himself that He alluded to
it. No doubt He was not so understood at the time.
Nevertheless such was the fact ; for we read, " But

He spoke of the temple of His body.  When, therefore, He was risen from the dead, His disciples re-
membered that He had said this; and they believed
the Scripture and the word which Jesus had said"
(John ii. 21, 22).

If I be correct in the above interpretation, the
following inferences will naturally suggest themselves :—

*First,* That the Lord would sometimes speak symbolically, and on such occasions would so express
Himself as if the symbol were the thing signified:

*Secondly,* That no inference as to His real meaning
can be safely adduced merely from the fact of His
remaining silent when He was aware that His language was misinterpreted: and,

*Thirdly,* That it is incumbent upon us carefully
to distinguish between the apparent and the real
meaning, for that, if from ignorance, prejudice, in-
attention, or no matter from what cause, we confound
the two to the prejudice of the truth, we incur the
danger of being included in the same category with
those whom the Evangelists describe as *false witnesses.*

Let us now proceed to the consideration of what I
have called the middle or third class of cases, viz.,
those occasions where the Lord condescended to
explain the sense in which He spoke, but in such
wise that His explanation was as mystical and in-

comprehensible to His hearers as the language He had used.

Of this class is the text we have selected for explanation, preliminary to considering the institution of the Holy Sacrament.

" Then Jesus said unto them, Verily, verily, I say unto you, Except ye eat the flesh of the Son of man, and drink His blood, ye have no life in you. Whoso eateth my flesh, and drinketh my blood, hath eternal life; and I will raise him up at the last day" (John vi. 53, 54).

There is this much in common between the above text and what is narrated in John ii. 19, namely, that all the various manuscripts agree in that, on the occasion mentioned in the second chapter of John, the words made use of by our Saviour (only substituting English for Greek) were, "Destroy this temple, and in three days I will raise it up;" and that He was understood to have spoken of the natural temple of Jerusalem. In like manner, all the manuscripts are substantially agreed that His words, on the second occasion, were, "Verily, verily, I say unto you, Except ye eat the flesh * of the Son of man, and, drink His blood, ye have no

---

* In the Peschito, what we translate from the Greek, "flesh" is "body:" "Unless you eat my *body*." See "The Syrian Churches and Gospels," by Etheridge. The Greek will also bear the same sense according to Parkhurst.

life in you. Whoso eateth my flesh, and drinketh my blood, hath eternal life;" and that He was understood by those who heard Him to speak of His natural flesh and blood.

But there is this distinction between them: In respect to the one, John expressly tells us that He spoke of the temple of His body. This explanation on the part of John was necessary to a correct understanding of the passage. But for it, we should to the present day have imagined Christ to have spoken of the temple of Jerusalem, for the Lord had not supplied any data whereby to correct our judgment. But John gives us no explanation of what Christ meant in respect to the eating of His flesh and the drinking of His blood. And for this sufficient reason, that the Lord himself had afforded those who had ears to hear the means of correctly interpreting Him.

*First,* Let us investigate what He did not mean. His words were, "Whoso eateth my flesh, and drinketh my blood, hath eternal life" (John vi. 54).

That the Lord did not thereby intend His natural flesh and His natural blood, follows from what He subsequently says.

In verses 57 and 58, He says, "As the living Father hath sent me, and I live by the Father; so he that eateth me, even he shall live by me. This

is that bread which came down from heaven: not
as your fathers did eat manna, and are dead: he
that eateth of this bread shall live for ever."*

Here, then, we learn that we are to eat Him in
the sense in which He lived by the Father, and what
that was He had explained on a former occasion,
—"I have meat to eat that ye know not of. My
meat is to do the will of Him that sent me, and
to finish His work" (John iv. 32 and 34); and, consistently with this, having told us that as He lived
by the Father, so we were to eat Him, He adds,
"This is that bread which came down from heaven:
not as your fathers did eat manna, and are dead:
he that eateth this bread shall live for ever."

"These things," we are told, "said He in the
synagogue as He taught in Capernaum" (ver. 59);
that is to say, in a mixed society, composed partly
of Jews and partly of His disciples: and mark the
different impressions His words made upon these
two classes of persons. When the Lord, in verse 51,
first hinted at the idea of their eating His flesh,
the *Jews* strove among themselves, saying, "How

---

* Mr Ainsley adopts the reading of verse 58, suggested by
Tischendorf in his note to our A. V.:—"He is the bread which
came down from heaven; not as the fathers did eat and have
died: he who eateth this bread shall live for ever." The Peschito
reads, "This is the bread which hath descended from heaven. Not
as was the manna that your fathers ate and are dead; he who
eateth this bread shall live for ever."

can this man give us His flesh to eat?" (ver. 52).
But when He afterwards explained that He did not
mean that they should eat His flesh, "as their
fathers did eat," His *disciples*, who were aware that
He often spoke in allegory, simply said, "This
is an hard saying; who can hear it?" (ver. 60).
"When Jesus knew in Himself that His disciples
murmured at it, He said unto them, Doth this
offend you?  What and if ye shall see the Son of
man ascend up to where He was before?  It is the
Spirit that quickeneth; the flesh profiteth nothing:
the words that *I have spoken* * unto you are spirit,
and are life" (ver. 63).

The following, as suggested Dr Adam Clarke,
appears to have been the reasoning of the Lord:—
"I have told you that you must eat my flesh and
drink my blood, and I have also told you that you
are not to eat my flesh and blood in the sense in
which your fathers ate in the wilderness.  If you
are puzzled at this, still more will you be puzzled

---

* In the Greek of our received versions, the expression is ἐγὼ
λαλῶ, *I speak*, in the present tense.  But many prefer to read ἐγὼ
λελάληκα, *have spoken*, in the past tense, for which see the authorities in Clarke's Commentary.  The pronouns are obviously
not in the original, and are not necessary to the understanding of
the passage; I have, therefore, omitted them.  The reading contended for by Dr Adam Clarke is also that of the Peschito, as
translated by Etheridge: "The words which I *have* spoken, they
are spirit, and they are life."  This is also the reading of the
Nitrian fragments, as translated by the late Dr Cureton.

when the time shall arrive, and most assuredly it will arrive, for you to see me taken away from you bodily, so that the eating of my flesh and the drinking of my blood will have become a physical impossibility ; inasmuch as, so far from their being eaten and drunk by men, they shall not even be found amongst them. But I am not speaking of my natural flesh. It is the spiritual sense that quickeneth ; the eating of the natural flesh profiteth nothing ; and the words I have spoken to you respecting my flesh and blood are to be interpreted spiritually, for they are spirit and life." (See Clarke's Com., *in loc.*)

His disciples, however, do not seem to have understood Him, for we are told that "from that time many of His disciples went back, and walked no more with Him" (ver. 66). Thereupon the Lord turned to His chosen apostles, to whom His language appears to have been quite as unintelligible as it was to the other of His disciples, and "said unto the twelve, Will ye also go away? Then Simon Peter answered Him, Lord, to whom shall we go? Thou hast the words of eternal life. And we believe, and are sure that thou art that Christ, the Son of the living God" (ver. 66-69).

During the whole of the Lord's ministry on earth, His apostles appear to have been men of inferior intellectual capacities, and in quickness of apprehen-

B

sion far below the average run of mankind. Often as our Saviour alluded to His resurrection, they were quite unable to realise the fact; and when it did occur, so little were they prepared for it, that it seems to have taken them all by surprise (John xx. 9). So it was even in matters in which nothing supernatural was involved. On the occasion of the Last Supper, the supper being ended, Jesus, among other things, said, "Verily, verily, I say unto you, That one of you shall betray me." This was said in the hearing of them all, who looked one on the other doubting of whom He spoke. At length, at the instigation of Peter, the disciple lying on Jesus' breast saith unto Him, "Lord, who is it? Jesus answered, He it is to whom I shall give a sop, when I have dipped it. And when He had dipped the sop, He gave it to Judas Iscariot, the son of Simon. And after the sop Satan entered into him. Then said Jesus unto him, That thou doest, do quickly. He then, having received the sop, went immediately out." And yet it did not occur to any one of the other disciples to suspect what it was that Christ alluded to when He accompanied the giving of the sop with the words, "That thou doest, do quickly." We are expressly told that "no man at the table knew for what intent He spake this unto him" (John xiii. 24–30).

We have therefore no reason to be surprised if, in

their hour of mental darkness, the apostles did not comprehend the obscure language of the Lord, when He told them they were to eat His flesh and drink His blood, but that they were not to eat it as their fathers had eaten manna; that, in fact, the flesh (that is to say, the natural flesh) profiteth nothing, and that the words He had spoken were spirit and life. But in the course of a short time a sudden change came over them, a change so sudden and so great as to be as irreconcilable with our ordinary experience of mental development as any of the miracles we read of are irreconcilable with our ordinary experience of the general laws of nature. For we are told that after the Lord's resurrection, " He opened their understandings, that they might understand the Scriptures" (Luke xxiv. 45) ; and certain it is, that from thenceforward, without any apparent effort, these men, who had previously been remarkably dull and slow of apprehension, were suddenly, and as it were, instinctively, enabled to take a full and comprehensive view of the entire scheme of Christianity. Hence it is, that what at first was obscure is no longer so, and with the aid of the additional light thrown upon the subject by the inspired commentaries of the Evangelists and the apostles, we are now in a position to perceive that when our Saviour commanded us to eat His flesh and to drink His blood, He was expressing Himself in mystical language, and that, whatever

may have been His real meaning, at all events He did
not intend to be understood as speaking of His natural
flesh and natural blood.

*Secondly*, Having, then, ascertained what it was
that the Lord did not mean, it only remains to investigate affirmatively what He did mean.

The process of eating, as applicable to the assimi-
lating of spiritual truths, was a figure of speech with
which the Jews had been familiar long before the
advent of the Lord. Towards the close of the second
chapter and the commencement of the third chapter
of Ezekiel, we read that the Almighty, having com-
missioned the prophet to expostulate with the children
of Israel, spoke as follows:—" And thou shalt speak
my words unto them, whether they will hear, or
whether they will forbear; for they are most rebellious. But thou, son of man, hear what I say unto
thee: Be not thou rebellious like unto that rebellious
house: open thy mouth, and eat that I give thee.
And when I looked, behold, an hand was sent unto
me; and, lo, a roll of a book was therein; and He
spread it before me; and it was written within and
without: and there was written therein lamentations,
and mourning, and woe. Moreover, He said unto
me, Son of man, eat that thou findest; eat this roll,
and go speak unto the house of Israel. So I opened
my mouth, and He caused me to eat that roll. And
He said unto me, Son of man, cause thy belly to eat

and fill thy bowels with that I give thee. Then did
I eat it; and it was in my mouth as honey for sweet-
ness." In a similar spirit, when the Lord's disciples
prayed Him, saying, "Master, eat; He said unto
them, I have meat to eat that ye know not of.
Therefore said the disciples, Hath any man brought
Him ought to eat? Jesus said unto them, My *meat*
is to do the will of Him that sent me, and to finish
His work" (John iv. 31–34). Not that the doing
of the will of Him that sent Him was meat in the
sense intended by His disciples. But, as was not
unusual with Him, when an ordinary question was
put to Him admitting of a spiritual interpretation,
He would often disregard the natural, and shape His
reply with a view to its spiritual sense.

Let any candid person bear in mind this peculiarity
of our Lord's speech, and he will perceive how little
reliance is to be placed on any isolated expressions,
however clear and definite, by themselves and apart
from the context, they may appear to be. Thus it
is that when we read, that " Whoso eateth my flesh
and drinketh my blood hath eternal life ($\zeta\omega\grave{\eta}\nu$
$ai\acute{\omega}\nu\iota o\nu$), and I will raise him up at the last day,"
if we limit ourselves to this isolated passage, and
interpret it according to the ordinary signification of
the words, it would seem as though the Lord really
contemplated our eating His natural flesh and
drinking His natural blood. We have only to com-

pare this passage with what He had previously said, and it becomes apparent that those who have *faith* in Christ are said to eat His flesh and drink His blood. "And this is the will of Him that sent me, that every one which seeth the Son, and believeth on Him, may have everlasting life ($\zeta\omega\grave{\eta}\nu$ $a\grave{\iota}\acute{\omega}\nu\iota o\nu$—precisely the same expression); and I will raise him up at the last day" (John vi. 40). From which it is obvious that, "to see and to believe in Christ," or, what amounts to the same thing, "*to have faith in Christ*," and "*to eat His flesh and drink His blood*," are convertible forms of expression, and might be substituted the one for the other.

That the above is not an accidental coincidence, but was really what the Lord intended, is so obviously the case, that it is difficult to conceive how the ingenuity of the most subtle intellect can have suggested a different reading.

The occasion of His delivering the address in which the passage of eating His flesh and drinking His blood occurs arose in this wise. The Lord had only a short time before performed the miracle of the multiplication of the loaves and fishes. After He had performed this miracle, He entered into a ship, and went over the sea to Capernaum, ; and on the following day the people who had been fed by Him, "also took shipping and came to Capernaum, seeking Jesus; and when they had found Him, they said

unto Him, Rabbi, when camest thou hither?" (John
vi. 1-25). Thereupon the Lord delivers that sub-
limely mystical discourse, towards the close of which
He tells us, " The words that I have spoken unto
you are spirit and are life." To the same effect is
what we also read in 2 Cor. iii. 6, where Paul also
cautions us against laying too much stress upon
the mere letter of the New Testament. His words
are, " Who also hath made us able ministers of
the New Testament; not of the letter, but of the
spirit: for the letter killeth, but the spirit giveth
life."

The Lord commences His discourse by telling
those who had followed Him, " Ye seek me, not
because ye saw the miracles, but because ye did eat
of the loaves and were filled" (John vi. 26). He
then tells them, " Labour not for the meat which
perisheth, but for that meat which endureth unto
everlasting life, which the Son of man shall give
unto you" (ver. 27). He is evidently here speaking of
food in a spiritual sense, though His hearers did not
so understand Him. " Then said they unto Him,
What shall we do that we might work the works of
God? Jesus answered and said unto them, This is
the work of God, that ye believe on Him whom He
has sent" (ver. 28, 29). Then they demanded of Him
some sign of His authority, and remind Him that
their fathers did eat manna in the desert. " Then

Jesus said unto them, Verily, verily, I say unto you,
Moses gave you not that bread from heaven ; but my
Father giveth you the *true bread* from heaven " (ver.
32) ; thus distinguishing between the two kinds of
food, the natural and the spiritual, which latter He
speaks of as *true bread*, in contradistinction to the
manna or bread their fathers had eaten in the desert.
" For the bread of God," He continues, " is He which
cometh down from heaven, and giveth life unto the
world.    Then said they unto Him,"—still at cross-
purposes as to His meaning,—" Lord, evermore give
us this bread.    And Jesus said unto them, *I am the*
*bread of life :* he that cometh to me shall never
hunger ; and he that believeth in me shall never
thirst " (ver. 33–35).    It cannot here fail to be observed, that though our Lord speaks of Himself as
*bread*, it is not to *ordinary bread* that He compares
Himself, but to the *bread of life*.    And He subsequently explains what He means by *bread of life*,
viz., faith in Him.    For, in verse 47, he says:
" Verily, verily, I say unto you, He that believeth in
me hath everlasting life ;" and immediately, in verse
48, " *I am the bread of life*."    At other times, He
would speak of Himself as living water ; as where
He said to the woman of Samaria, " Whosoever
drinketh of the water that I shall give him, shall
never thirst ; but the water that I shall give him
shall be a well of water springing up into everlasting

life" (John iv. 14). And, again: "If any man thirst,
let him come unto me and drink. He that believeth
on me, as the Scripture hath said, out of his belly
shall flow rivers of living water. But," adds John,
"this spake He of the Spirit, which they that believe
on Him should receive" (John vii. 37-39). On the
present occasion, He assimilates Himself, not to living water, but to the bread of life, for which He
afterwards substitutes His flesh. "I am the *living
bread* which came down from heaven: if any man
eat of *this bread,* he shall live for ever; and the
bread" (that is to say, the *living bread*) "that I will
give is my *flesh,* which I will give for the *life of
the world*" (John vi. 51). But whether He speaks
of the bread of life, of living water, or of His
flesh and blood, they are only so many different
forms of expression, indicative of the same thing,
viz., the all-sufficient efficacy of faith: by which is
not to be understood a mere unproductive assent of
the understanding, for we are told that the devils
believe and tremble, but that full and implicit confidence in the Lord, that can only exist where there
is a cordial reception of, and strict obedience to, the
gospel doctrines; or, in other words, an entire sur-
rendering of the individual to the will of God. (See
πιστεύω, Parkhurst.) Let any person compare the
following passages, and he will at once perceive that
the above is what the Lord intended under the ap-

propriate figure of eating His flesh and drinking His blood:—

"Verily, verily, I say unto you, He that heareth my word, and believeth on Him that sent me, *hath everlasting life*, and shall not come into condemnation; but *is passed* from death unto life" (John v. 24).

"And this is the will of Him that sent me, that every one that seeth the Son, and believeth on Him, may have everlasting life: *and I will raise him up at the last day*" (John vi. 40).

"Verily, verily, I say unto you, He that believeth on me hath everlasting life" (John vi. 47).

"Verily, verily, I say unto you, If a man keep my saying, he shall never see death" (John viii. 51).

"And how *I kept back nothing that was profitable*,* but have showed you, and have taught you publicly, and from house to house, testifying both to the Jews, and also to the Greeks, repentance towards God, and

"This said Jesus unto them, Verily, verily, I say unto you, Except ye eat the flesh of the Son of man, and drink His blood, *ye have no life* in you" (John vi. 53).

"Whoso eateth my flesh, and drinketh my blood, *hath* eternal life" (the same as is elsewhere rendered everlasting life); "and *I will raise him up at the last day*" (John vi. 54).

* There is no allusion in the Epistles of Paul to the eating of Christ's flesh.

faith toward our Lord Jesus Christ" (Acts xx. 20, 21).

"What must I do to be saved? Believe on the Lord Jesus Christ, and thou shalt be saved, and thy house" (Acts xvi. 30, 31).

"And this is His commandment, That we should believe on the name of His Son Jesus Christ, and love one another, as He gave us commandment. And he that keepeth His commandments *dwelleth in Him, and He in him*" (1 John iii. 23, 24).

"Whosoever shall confess that Jesus is the Son of God, *God dwelleth in him, and he in God*" (1 John iv. 15).

"He that eateth my flesh and drinketh my blood, *dwelleth in me, and I in him* (John vi. 56).

Hence, then, from comparing the words of our Lord in John vi. 53, 54, with what He himself had previously and subsequently said on the same and other occasions, as well as with what we read in the writings of the inspired penmen, it clearly follows that, when the Lord speaks of our eating His flesh and drinking His blood, He does not mean that we are to eat His natural flesh and drink His natural blood, but is symbolically describing the spiritual operation of the Holy Ghost through faith in Christ.

# CHAPTER II.

I HAD written the former chapter before I had had
an opportunity of perusing the celebrated "Lectures
on the Principal Doctrines and Practices of the
Catholic Church," by the late Cardinal Wiseman,*
and had no intention of pursuing the subject any
further. But the friends for whom I had written it,
subsequently lent me a copy of the lectures, with a
view to my answering those of them that treated on
the doctrine of transubstantiation.

The lectures are conceived with great ability, and
are written in a very fascinating style. They are
therefore well calculated to make a favourable impression upon those who are not in the habit of closely
analysing an argument. There are sixteen lectures
in all; but it is in the three concluding ones, viz.,
the 14th, 15th and 16th, that the subject of transubstantiation is treated of, and of these three, the
one, with which we are at present more immediately
concerned, is the fourteenth, which is devoted to the
discussion of the sixth of John.

* Published by the Catholic Publishing and Bookselling Company
(Limited), 33 New Bond Street, 1867, second edition.

The early portion of this lecture is principally occupied with an exposition of the principles of interpretation that Cardinal Wiseman proposes for the guidance of his hearers. So far as these general principles are concerned they need not detain us. As *general principles*, their propriety may, with certain verbal modifications, be safely conceded without materially affecting the substantial merits of any matter in controversy between us.

Similarly, Cardinal Wiseman's learned dissertation on the force of the expression " to eat a man's flesh," is more interesting and instructive than of importance to the argument. " It is remarkable," says Cardinal Wiseman, " that in Syro-Chaldaic there is no expression for to accuse or calumniate, except *to eat a morsel of the person calumniated;* so much so, that in the Syriac version of Scripture, which was made one or two centuries after our Saviour, there is no name given throughout to the devil, which in the Greek version signifies *the accuser*, or calumniator, but the ' eater of flesh' " (Lect. xiv. 152) : and, indeed, I think it may be fairly admitted that the expression " to eat a man's flesh " was never employed among the Jews in a *purely figurative* sense, except as a term of reproach. But I hope to show that the Lord was not speaking in ordinary figurative language; though, in substituting a different meaning to His words, I shall not feel myself limited to an interpretation that was likely to have been correctly understood by His audience. For as I read what occurred, it seems to me that there were none then present who either did, or who were even capable of understanding Him ; and that He was Himself fully aware of the fact.

Cardinal Wiseman's argument ultimately resolves itself into the following fundamental propositions, viz. :—

First, That though from verse 27 to verse 50, both inclusive, all parties, both Protestants and Catholics, are agreed that our Saviour is to be taken as speaking of faith, at verse 50 or somewhere thereabouts, a change takes place in our Saviour's discourse, and that from that moment we are not to understand Him as speaking of faith, but solely the real eating of His body and drinking of His blood sacramentally in the Eucharist (Lect. xiv. 140).

Secondly, That whenever the Jews took the words of our Lord literally, and He meant them figuratively, He invariably explained His meaning, and told them they were wrong in taking literally what He meant to be figurative (Lect. xiv. 160–162).

Thirdly, That whenever the Jews understood Him rightly in a literal sense, and objected to the doctrine proposed, He repeated the very phrases which had given offence ; and that the texts in question fall within this last class (Lect. xiv. 162).

Such are the several issues raised by Cardinal Wiseman, and on which he has staked the validity of his argument. I propose to examine them *seriatim*. But before doing so, it is necessary to clear the first of them of a verbal ambiguity.

What does Cardinal Wiseman mean by the "real eating of His body and drinking of His blood *sacramentally* in the Eucharist?" The entire force of the sentence apparently depends upon the sense we attach to that qualifying word, *sacramentally*. There is no class of Protestants with whom I am acquainted, who recognise the sanctity of the Lord's Supper, that does not hold that we *sacramentally* eat the body and drink the blood of Christ. At all events, it is so taught in the Catechism of the Church of England. "What is the outward part or sign of the Lord's Supper?—Bread and wine, which the Lord hath commanded to be received. What is the inward part or thing signified?—The body and blood of Christ, which are verily and indeed taken and received by the faithful in the Lord's Supper. What are the benefits whereof we are the partakers thereby?—The strengthening and refreshing of our souls by the body and blood of Christ, as our bodies are by the bread and wine." This is even more fully explained in our Articles of Religion. "The Supper of the Lord is not only a sign of the love that Christians ought to have among themselves one to another; but rather is a sacrament of our redemption by Christ's death: insomuch as that to such as rightly, worthily, and with faith receive the same, the bread which we break is a partaking of the body of Christ; and likewise the cup of blessing is a partaking of the blood of Christ;" and further, "The body of Christ is given, taken, and eaten in the Supper, only after an heavenly and spiritual manner. And the mean whereby the body of Christ is received and eaten in the Supper is faith." (See Art. xxviii.) If the above be what Cardinal Wiseman means to convey by "eating and drinking the body and blood of Christ SACRAMENTALLY," then he and I so entirely agree that any further discussion would be only a waste of words.

But if Cardinal Wiseman intended thereby the proposition he had originally undertaken to prove, viz., that in the Blessed Eucharist that which was originally bread and wine is, by consecration, changed into the substance of the body and blood of our Lord, together with His soul and divinity, in other words, His complete and entire person, as defined by the Council of Trent, in such case the word SACRAMENT-ALLY is simply superfluous, and adds nothing to the force or meaning of the sentence. (See Lect. xiv., p. 136).

The proposition we are now about to investigate is simply this:—Admitting that from verse 27 to verse 50, both inclusive, of the sixth chapter of John, the Lord, under the symbol of the true bread or the bread of life, is to be understood as figuratively speaking of faith, there are grounds for supposing that in verse 51, He suddenly changes His style from the figurative to the literal, and that what He says of eating His flesh and drinking His blood, is to be understood of His natural flesh and blood.

It seems to be conceded by Cardinal Wiseman that there are no express indications of such a change; that the precise point of departure is so obscurely defined, that whilst it is generally supposed to occur at verse 51, he himself is inclined to place it at verse 48, and has given his reasons at length in his "Lectures on the Real Presence." (See Lect. xiv., p. 142.) I do not propose to lay more stress upon this admission than it is justly entitled to. That our Saviour did thus frequently alternate between the spiritual and literal is no doubt the case, though the instance from Matthew xxiv. which Cardinal Wiseman has selected by way of illustration has no bearing on the subject. But were it otherwise, it would fail to show that there is *no* weight in the objection. The objection, though not conclusive, would be still entitled not only to *some* but to *considerable* weight. For if we are to interpret the Scriptures in accordance with the canon of interpretation as propounded by Cardinal Wiseman

(p. 137), it would necessarily be in the highest degree improbable, and in direct contravention of the rule which he says is the groundwork of all the science of interpretation,—that our Saviour, who had just been speaking of Himself as the bread of life, should, in the '51st verse, going on with precisely the same expressions, make such a complete transition in the subject of His discourse (p. 140). But not to dwell at greater length upon this point, I shall content myself with accepting for whatever they may be worth the two following admissions on the part of Cardinal Wiseman :—

First, That from verse 27 to verse 50 of John vi., the Lord is figuratively speaking of faith ; and,

Secondly, That there is no express indication of a subsequent transition from the figurative to the literal, or any marks whereby accurately to define the precise point of transition, supposing it to have occurred.

All parties, both Protestant and Catholic, are agreed, says Cardinal Wiseman, that from the 26th verse so far as about the 50th, our Saviour's discourse is about faith (p. 140). It is also admitted by Cardinal Wiseman that, during the whole of that interval, what the Lord says of bread under the various forms of " meat which endureth unto everlasting life," " bread from heaven," " true bread from heaven," " bread of God," or " bread of life," is to be construed figuratively (I should prefer the phrase *spiritually*) of faith. For, as he justly observes, and refers to a variety of references in proof of what he says,—" The ideas of giving bread and of partaking of food were commonly applied to teaching and receiving instruction" (p. 143). " Therefore, when our Saviour simply addresses the Jews, speaking of food whereof they are to partake, the Cardinal has no difficulty in supposing that He could be understood by all as referring to faith in Him and His teaching" (p. 144).

But if this be so, it affords a most complete and satisfactory answer to the critical objections founded on the peculiar wording of the 35th verse, as alleged by Cardinal Wiseman. He says, " Throughout the first part of this chapter, if you read it carefully over, you will not once find our Saviour allude to the idea of eating. He does not once speak of eating 'the bread which came down from heaven.' On the contrary, in verse 35, He actually violates the ordinary rhetorical proprieties of language to avoid this harsh and unnatural figure" (p. 144).

The first question that suggests itself is, whether the above be a correct exposition of what had occurred? The answer to which is, that it is partially correct, but substantially incorrect; that is to say, it is so far true that the Lord had not expressly, and in so many words, mentioned *the eating of the bread which came down from heaven;* but so far from our

Saviour not having once alluded to it throughout the former part of the chapter, it is unmistakably implied in everything He had said upon the subject. And, indeed, were this not the case, there could have been no " violation of the ordinary rhetorical proprieties of language." The alleged rhetorical impropriety of language consisted in this, that whereas the Lord had heretofore been speaking of the *bread of life* as the food they ought to eat, and having afterwards described Himself as being the bread of life, He ought, according to the rules of rhetorical propriety, to have followed up the announcement with, " *Come and eat, or receive me,* and ye shall never hunger ; " but instead of that, He simply says, " *Come to me,* and ye shall never hunger." Hence it follows that if the Lord had not before alluded to eating the bread of life, there would have been no violation of rhetorical proprieties.

But, secondly, was there any violation of the rhetorical proprieties of language ?

Before investigating this point, I cannot help remarking, that the proposition itself has a somewhat grating sound upon the ears. When we consider who it is whose words we are criticising, namely, the Lord Jesus Christ, there is an approximation to irreverence in the form of expression, " *violating the rhetorical proprieties of language.*" And the reason assigned for His so doing makes the matter

worse; for it is contrary to the whole tenor of our
Saviour's life to suppose Him capable of accom-
modating His language to meet the prejudices of
those around Him.

But how does the case stand? It is admitted
on all hands that the *bread of life* means faith in
Christ, and that to *eat the bread of life* means to
have faith in Christ. And surely the same thing
is meant by the expression as used by the Lord in
verse 35 of " *he that cometh to me.*" In verse 37
He says, " All that the Father giveth to me shall
*come* to me; and him that *cometh to me* I will in no
wise cast out." In the 44th and 45th verses He says,
" No man can come to me, except the Father, which
hath sent me, draw him: and I will raise him up
at the last day "—(precisely the same as He had said
of those who had *faith in Him*, ver. 40).—" It is
written in the prophets, And they shall be all taught
of God. Every man therefore that hath heard, and
hath learned of the Father, *cometh to me.*" But
not only in the sixth chapter of John, but throughout the entire Gospels, the expression *coming to
Christ* is synonymously used for *faith in Christ.*
When, therefore, the Lord said, " I am the bread of
life: he that cometh to me shall never hunger," He
virtually said, " I am the bread of life: he that eateth
me shall never hunger," the two forms of speech,
" coming to me " and " eating me," being, spiritually

considered, convertible terms, and consequently there was no violation of the rhetorical proprieties of language in substituting the one for the other.

The next point commented upon by Cardinal Wiseman is what we read in the 41st and 42d verses, relative to the murmuring of the Jews, because they understood the Lord to have said that *He was the bread which came down from heaven.* Cardinal Wiseman remarks, that their objection was not so much to His calling Himself bread, as to His saying that He had come down from heaven. I cannot assent to this, because I am unable to disconnect the 42d from the 41st verse; to do so, would be to suppose that John had misrepresented the facts of the case. For he expressly tells us that they murmured because He said, " I am the bread which came down from heaven." Hence I infer, that though in the 42d verse no mention is made of bread in the words reported to have been used, nevertheless, from the general tenor and tone of the remarks, the Jews were obviously alluding to the bread that came down from heaven. What, then, is the explanation of their difficulty, and what the force of their objection ?

They had witnessed the miracle of the loaves, and fancied that Christ, through the favour of God, or possibly through the agency of magic,* was in posses-

* The value of magical books, surrendered by converts to Christianity alone, was estimated at the enormous sum of 50,000 pieces of silver. (See Acts xix. 19.)

sion of a secret whereby He could indefinitely multiply natural food. But they imagined that what He had done He had accomplished by natural means. On the other hand, there was a tradition amongst them, that in ages long since past, their ancestors were fed by *bread from heaven.* "Our fathers did eat manna in the desert; as it is written, He gave them *bread from heaven* to eat" (ver. 31). This was the only *bread from heaven* they had ever heard of. When, therefore, Christ said that He was the bread which came down from heaven, they thought He thereby claimed to Himself the credit of having supplied the bread or manna which their fathers had eaten in the desert centuries before. Whereupon they murmured among themselves, because, as they argued, He could not have existed in those days, for that they had known Him from His infancy, and identified Him as Jesus the son of Joseph, whose father and mother they were acquainted with.

The force of the objection was precisely similar to that which the Jews, on a subsequent occasion, took when the Lord said, "Your father Abraham rejoiced to see my day: and he saw it, and was glad. Then said the Jews unto Him, Thou art not yet fifty years old, hast thou seen Abraham?" Whereupon the Lord condescends to explain that HE WAS GOD. "Jesus said unto them, Verily, verily, I say unto you, Before Abraham was, I AM" (John viii. 56–58).

On the present occasion He did not stoop to notice their difficulty, but simply told them not to murmur amongst themselves. "Jesus therefore answered and said unto them, Murmur not among yourselves" (John vi. 43).

According to Cardinal Wiseman, the Lord employed no less than seven or eight verses in removing the difficulty that occasioned the murmuring among the Jews; but he does not attempt to show how what subsequently fell from our Saviour operated as an answer to the objection they had raised. (See p. 145). On the other hand, I say that He made no effort to remove their difficulty; that He treated it with contemptuous indifference; and that what He subsequently said had no reference to it in the most distant degree.

The objection on the part of the Jews, according to Cardinal Wiseman's view, was to their having understood the Lord, in speaking of Himself, to have said that He came down from heaven, whereas they were themselves personally acquainted with His origin, and of their own knowledge knew Him to be no other than Jesus the son of Joseph. The only natural and obvious answer to the above objection would have been for Christ to have explained how, consistently with what they had known of His earthly origin, He nevertheless was justified in saying that He had come down from heaven. But instead of that, He tells them, "No man can come to me, except the Father, which hath sent me, draw him: and I will raise him up at the last day;" which was obviously beside the question, and no answer to it at all.

But take the other view, and everything assumes a perfect consistency.

In the 35th verse Jesus had said, " I am the bread of life." He had also told them, " He that cometh to me shall never hunger."

Having stated these two propositions, He enlarges more particularly upon the second of the two. The Jews, however, fancy they have caught Him in a trap; for that if what He had said were true, He must have existed in the days of their ancestors, whereas they knew Him to have been born in the ordinary course of nature only a few years ago. They accordingly began to talk among themselves. Whereupon the Lord tells them to desist from murmuring. " Murmur not among yourselves." As if He had said, Do not interrupt me, but attend to what I am saying. Silence being restored, He resumes His discourse from where He had left it off, and, after describing the spiritual advantages in store for those who come to Him, proceeds to explain that "no man can come to me, except the Father, which hath sent me, draw Him;" nor does He change the subject till the close of the 47th verse, when He reverts to and repeats

what He had said in the first division of the 35th
verse: "I am that bread of life" (ver. 48).

If the above be a correct analysis of what occurred,
—of which the reader must judge for himself—it follows that Cardinal Wiseman misconceived the purport
of the narration, and was under a misapprehension in
supposing that what fell from our Saviour was in
answer to the murmuring of the Jews.

Having thus disposed of these preliminary difficulties, we now come to what constitutes the principal
question at issue between Protestants and Roman
Catholics, viz., whether there be any indications of
a sudden change of style from the figurative to the
literal in what fell from the Lord subsequently to
verse 49 ?

In the investigation of this point I shall discard
from consideration all those rules of interpretation
the force of which depends upon inferences deduced
from the course we ourselves should probably have
pursued ; such, for instance, as the following :—It is
obvious that when Christ spoke of the eating of His
flesh, the Jews in general understood Him to speak
of His natural flesh. It is also equally clear that His
disciples were quite unable to understand what He
meant. Their words were, "This is a hard saying;
who can hear it?" I do not agree with Cardinal
Wiseman in the interpretation he puts upon these
words. He says, it is as if the disciples had said,

"This is a disagreeable and odious proposition. It is impossible any longer to associate with a man who teaches us such revolting doctrines as these " (p. 165). On the contrary, it appears to me that what they intended to convey was, that the language of the Lord involved some hidden mystery which they could not unravel. But, says Cardinal Wiseman, " can we possibly imagine that, if He had been speaking all this time in figures, and they had misunderstood Him, He would permit them to be lost for ever, in consequence of their refusing to believe imaginary doctrines, which He never meant to teach them ? " My answer is, that we cannot test the actions of Infinite Wisdom by the notions of propriety as entertained by finite understandings. Everything connected with the origin of sin, the consequent fall of man, and the process by which his redemption is effected, is hopelessly beyond our powers of comprehension. It is the same with the moral government of God apart from Christianity. But inasmuch as we are necessitated to elect between a belief in the existence or in the non-existence of a God, so are we bound in reason to follow one or the other hypothesis to its legitimate consequences. In like manner is it in respect to Christianity according as we believe the Lord Jesus Christ to have been, or not to have been, of a divinely superhuman nature.

That there are a variety of occurrences in nature

that apparently clash with our notions of infinite
mercy, is unquestionably true.   Nevertheless, if we
assume that such events have happened, in obedience
to the decrees of a Being all-powerful and infinitely
merciful, we are necessarily compelled to the conclusion that, were we enabled, which we are not, to
penetrate the councils of God, it would at once be
apparent to us that everything had been ordained by
His infinite wisdom in the most perfect manner.   So,
also, if we believe the personal description of the
Lord Jesus Christ as recorded in the volume of the
sacred law, all questions as to why He expressed
Himself in one way rather than another, in reference
to matters on which we have positive evidence of
what He did, are frivolous in the extreme.   " Man,"
says Bacon, " being the servant and interpreter of
nature, can do and understand so much, and so much
only, as he has observed in fact or in thought of
nature ;  beyond this, He neither knows anything nor
can do anything" (Nov. Org.)   So, also, is it in the
interpretation of matters connected with the sayings
or doings of Christ.   In both cases our inquiries are
restricted to an investigation of, not what we fancy
ought to have been the course pursued, but what,
under the ascertained facts, did actually occur.

   It is admitted on all hands that when our Saviour
said, in the 35th verse, " I am the bread of life," He
is to be understood as figuratively or spiritually speak-

ing of faith under the symbol of "the bread of life."
It is, also, *argumentatively conceded* * that a similarly
figurative or spiritual sense attaches to the same form
of expression when repeated in verse 48, "I am
that bread of life."

Taking, then, this as our starting-point, the Lord
proceeds, in verse 49, to remind the Jews that their
fathers did eat manna in the wilderness and are dead;
and in verse 50 He contrasts the effect of eating
manna or natural food with the effect of eating the
bread of life. "This is the bread of life which
cometh down from heaven, that a man may eat
thereof and not die." Up to this point it is, for the
purpose of the present argument, conceded that the
Lord is to be taken as expressing Himself in figurative
or spiritual language. But it should be borne in
mind, that there is no indication from which we can
infer that the Jews understood Him to be so speaking.
On the contrary, what was then most prominent in
their minds was the miracle they had witnessed of
the loaves, and from which they imagined He had
some mystical knowledge by means of which He
could multiply *natural food.* "Verily, verily, I say
unto you, Ye seek me, not because ye saw the miracles,
but because ye did eat of the loaves, and were filled"

* I say *argumentatively conceded,* because, at the commencement
of page 142, Cardinal Wiseman says he is strongly led to suppose
that the transition from the literal to the figurative takes place at
verse 48.

(ver. 26). From the whole tenor of what subsequently followed, nothing can be more obvious than that the Jews, throughout the whole of the Lord's discourse, misconceived the purport of what He said, and when He spoke of the *bread of life*, imagined that what He said had reference to *natural bread.*

Hence, then, we have arrived at these two points, of which the one is conceded, and must therefore be assumed as indisputable; the other is the natural inference from the previous portion of the sixth chapter, viz. :—

First, That what the Lord said, alluding to the bread of life, in verse 50, " This is the bread which cometh down from heaven, that a man may eat thereof and not die," is to be understood figuratively or spiritually of the operation of faith, under the symbol of eating the bread of life;

Secondly, That the Jews did not so understand it, but thought it referred to the eating of natural bread.

Let us now take the first portion of the next verse, and let us for a moment pause there. " I am the living bread which came down from heaven; if any man eat of this bread, he shall live for ever."*

Surely, if the Lord had stopped here, there would

---

* According to the Codex Sinaiticus, " I am the living bread : if any man eat of my bread he shall live for ever : the bread that I will give for the life of the world is my flesh." A. V. by Tischendorf. Note.

have been no indication of a change from the figurative or spiritual to the literal. Thus far what is said in the 51st verse had been included in verses 48 and 50. In fact it is only a condensing of those two verses, omitting the intermediate verse 49, as will appear if we place those two verses in juxtaposition : thus—

Ver. 48 and 50. "I am that bread of life. This is the bread which came down from heaven, that a man may eat thereof and not die."

Ver. 51. "I am the living bread which came down from heaven : if any man eat of this bread, he shall live for ever."

The sentiment in the two cases is precisely the same, though slightly varied in form ; and consequently, if the one be to be taken figuratively or spiritually, so of necessity must the other.

But the 51st verse did not stop where we have supposed it to have done ; it proceeds a step further, and substitutes His *flesh* for the *bread* He had been speaking of. "And the bread" (that is to say, the bread of life, figuratively or spiritually representing faith) "that I will give is my flesh, which I will give for the life of the world." Is it not obvious that, if faith be synonymous with bread, it must also be synonymous with flesh, seeing that the Lord has declared the one to be the same as the other? But to proceed. Having substituted His flesh for the bread of which He had been speaking, He pursues

the simile under its altered form ; and whereas He
had previously told them that they must eat the
bread of life, He now tells them they must eat His
flesh and drink His blood, and continues this train
of thought from the close of verse 51 to the beginning
of verse 57, when He reverts to His original figure,
and, in verse 58, tells them, " This " (that is to say,
His body and blood) " is that bread which came down
from heaven."

But how does Cardinal Wiseman grapple with the
difficulty suggested by the 58th verse ?  The answer
is, that he does not even attempt to grapple with it.
He could not.  It is so fatal to the issue he had
raised, that he felt his safest course was to divert
attention from it, and, with the skill of a practised
advocate, he has omitted all notice of it, as well as
of the other two explanatory verses, 62 and 63.

The argument, then, resolves itself into this: In
verse 51, Christ in substance says that He is the
living bread which cometh down from heaven ; that
they must eat of this bread, and that it is His flesh.

In verse 53 and following, He tells them that they
must eat His flesh and drink His blood.

In verse 58 He says, that " This " (that is to say,
His flesh and blood) " is that bread which came down
from heaven."

Hence it follows, that if the bread that came down
from heaven is to be understood as figuratively

or spiritually descriptive of faith, precisely a similar figurative or spiritual meaning must attach to His flesh and blood.

It only remains to investigate the applicability of the *second and third tests* propounded by Cardinal Wiseman, namely,—

First, That where our Lord meant to be taken figuratively, and the Jews *wrongly* took His words in their *crude literal sense*, and objected to the DOCTRINE, He invariably corrected them, and explained that He did not mean to be taken literally, but in a figurative sense (Lect. xiv., p. 162).

Secondly, Whenever the Jews understood Him *rightly* in a *literal sense*, and objected to the *doctrine* proposed, He repeated the very phrases which had given offence (p. 162).

I accept the above rules as a sufficient test whereby to determine whether the Lord were speaking figuratively or literally, with this addition to the second rule, viz., He repeats the phrase which had given offence, *without explaining that He did not mean to be taken literally, but in a spiritual sense.* These additional words only give completeness to the rule. For it cannot matter in what order an explanation is given. The meaning is equally obvious, at whatever part of the same discourse the explanation is supplied.

Subject to the above, I accept the test, and admit

D

that our Lord was understood by the Jews to have
been speaking literally.

The only point, therefore, at issue is, "Under
which of the above rules does the present case fall?"
Cardinal Wiseman says it comes under the second;
I say it falls under the first.

Cardinal Wiseman puts his point thus:

> PROPOSITION....."And the bread which I will give is MY
> FLESH, for the life of the world."
>
> OBJECTION......"How can this man give us HIS FLESH
> to eat?"
>
> ANSWER........."Amen, amen, I say unto you, Unless you
> eat THE FLESH of the SON of man, and
> drink HIS BLOOD, ye shall not have
> life."

To which I reply, if Christ had only said what you
quote from Him, your case would have been proved,
and I should be out of court.   But He said a great
deal more; and according to every rule of fair construction, if you rely upon a part of what a witness
says, you are bound to give the whole of what he
said.   Had you done so, you would have found that,
though the explanation was deferred, it was not
omitted.   True it is, the Lord did not allow the murmuring of the Jews to interrupt His then train of
thought; but He bore it in mind, and obviated their
difficulty before He concluded.   Let us arrange the
sentences according to the order of ideas as observed

by Christ, and the case will range itself under the
first rule :

PROPOSITION...." And the bread which I shall give is my
flesh, for the life of the world. Amen,
amen, I say unto you, Unless you eat
of the flesh of the Son of man, and
drink His blood, ye shall not have life
in you." And so on to the close of
verse 56.

OBJECTION......"How can this man give us His flesh to
eat ?"

ANSWER........" As the living Father hath sent me, and
I live by the Father : so he that eateth
me, even he shall live by me. This
is that bread which came down from
heaven : not as your fathers did eat
manna, and are dead : he that eateth
this bread shall live for ever. Ye shall
see the Son of man ascend up where
He was before.* It is the Spirit that
quickeneth ; the flesh profiteth nothing : the words that I have spoken
unto you are spirit and are life."

The difficulty in realising the import of the mystical language of sixth John principally arises from our
not sufficiently distinguishing between the natural
and spiritual. Cardinal Wiseman, throughout his
argument, assumes, that in what the Lord said about
eating His flesh and drinking His blood, if not to
be understood of His natural flesh and blood, He

* The 62d verse is evidently an affirmative proposition put
interrogatively.

must be considered as speaking figuratively. That, however, is to take a very limited and superficial view of the subject; for we are assured that there is a natural body, and there is a spiritual body (1 Cor. xv. 44); and, consequently, the one must of necessity be as complete an entity as the other. But there is this difference, that whereas the natural body is sustained by natural food, the spiritual body is sustained by spiritual food. Thus it is that bread, in its ordinary signification, is a proper sustenance for the natural body; but the food of the Spirit is bread from heaven. And the same form of speech is equally and literally applicable to both. So that when Christ said to His disciples that He had meat that they knew not of, and defined what He meant by " My meat is to do the will of Him that sent me, and to finish His work" (John iv. 32–34), He was not speaking figuratively, but literally, viz., that the food of the Spirit literally consisted in doing the will of God. In like manner, when He afterwards described the intimate but mystical union that would exist between Himself and true members of His Church, He describes Himself as the BREAD OF LIFE, and tells His disciples to eat His flesh and drink His blood: but immediately explains to them, that it is the Spirit that quickeneth; that the flesh (i.e., the natural flesh) profiteth nothing; and that the words He had spoken were spirit and life (John vi. 62,

63). So also Ezekiel was commanded to eat the roll (Ezek. iii. 1, and following verses) ; and John was told to eat the little book (Rev. x. 9). Whereas Adam, on the other hand, was forbidden to eat of the tree of the knowledge of good and evil.* In all these several instances, and in a variety of others of similar import, the same principle is involved, and are all to be understood in a literal, as contradistinguished from a figurative sense. For inasmuch as by eating natural food we appropriate what we eat, so that it becomes a part of our natural selves, by eating spiritual food, we similarly appropriate what we eat, and it becomes a part of our spiritual selves. And thus it is that when Christ tells us to eat His flesh and drink His blood, He virtually tells us spiritually to appropriate to ourselves His divine humanity, whereby the faithful become one with Him, and are collectively spoken of as being *His body.* " Now ye are the body of Christ, and members in particular " (1 Cor. xii. 27).

That the Lord should have been misinterpreted by those who heard Him, was to have been expected in the case of illiterate men, who seem to have been incapable of realising a spiritual idea, and whose misapprehensions are all of them reducible to the

---

* That is, he was forbidden to appropriate to himself, as if it originated in him, what in truth he had derived from God; and so, in his self-conceit, to be " as God, knowing good and evil."

same category, *the taking of our Lord to have spoken in a natural, instead of in a spiritual sense.* " Why do ye not understand my speech ? because ye cannot hear my word" (John viii. 43).   But that, in the present day, highly-educated individuals should persist in so interpreting Him, and, when He speaks of our eating His flesh and drinking His blood, should exhaust their energies in a vain endeavour to prove that He intended His natural flesh and His natural blood, is beyond all comparison the most extraordinary instance upon record of mental obliquity.

# PART THE SECOND.

———◆———

"NULLI DUBIUM ESSE POTEST, SI NIHIL IN EUCHARISTIA PRETER
PANEM SIT, QUIN TOTA ECCLESIA, JAM PER XV. ANNOS CENTENARIOS,
IDOLATRA FUERIT; AC, PROINDE, QUOTQUOT ANTE NOS HOC SACRA-
MENTUM ADORAVERUNT, OMNES AD UNUM ESSE DAMNATOS: NAM
CREATURAM PANIS ADORAVERINT CREATORIS LOCO."—*From the Works
of Cardinal Fisher, quoted by Faber in his "Difficulties of Romanism."*

# CHAPTER I.

In the former Part, I have endeavoured to explain the sixth chapter of John, and to controvert Cardinal Wiseman's interpretation of it in his fourteenth lecture. Strictly speaking, the fourteenth of Cardinal Wiseman's lectures is introductory to the two following lectures, and only indirectly touches upon the doctrine of transubstantiation; for the subject of transubstantiation does not arise in the sixth of John, which merely narrates a remarkable discourse of the Lord during the early days of His earthly ministry, long before the institution of the Last Supper.

We now come to the consideration of the fifteenth lecture, in which the subject of transubstantiation does properly arise; and as Roman Catholics profess to attach so much importance to the precise form of words made use of by the Lord, the exigencies of the argument suggest the propriety of ascertaining what they really were.

I have already observed that there are three of the Evangelists who have described what occurred on the occasion of the Last Supper (Matt. xxvi., Mark xiv., and Luke xxii.) ; and on comparing these several accounts the one with the others, we shall find that no two of them are in perfect agreement. The two first approximate to each other, but the third seems to have supplemented what they had omitted ; for whilst Matthew and Mark read, " This is my body," Luke says the words were, " This is my body, *which is given for you: this do in remembrance of me*" (Luke xxii. 19). And in speaking of the cup, according to Matthew, the Lord said, " This is my blood of the New* Testament, which is shed for many for the remission of sins". (Matt. xxvi. 28). In Mark, " This is my blood of the New Testament, which is shed for many " (Mark xiv. 24) ; and according to Luke, " This cup is the New Testament in my blood, which is shed for you " (Luke xxii. 20).

These several accounts are so substantially the same, or at all events so easily reconcilable, that their verbal disagreements only assume an importance from the undue weight attached by Roman Catholics

---

* *New* Testament. The word *new* in this and other similar texts is generally omitted by the best Greek authorities.

to the form of institution as given in Matthew, and their treating it as if it were identical with what we read in Luke.

Cardinal Wiseman, having adopted for his text the account as given by Matthew xxvi., casually remarks, " You are aware that the same circumstances are related, and very nearly the same words used, by two other Evangelists, and also by St Paul in his first Epistle to the Corinthians. It is not necessary to read over the passages in them all, because it is with reference to words common to all that I have principally to speak this evening" (Lect. xv., p. 174). Let us see whether this be really so.

In Matthew we read, " And while they were at supper, Jesus took bread, and blessed and gave to His disciples, and said, Take ye and eat; this is my body. And taking the chalice, He gave thanks, and gave to them, saying, Drink ye all of this, for this is my blood of the New Testament, which shall be shed for many for the remission of sins" * (Matt. xxvi. 26, 28).

" We have here," says Cardinal Wiseman, "two

---

* The above is as quoted by Cardinal Wiseman, who adopts the reading of the Vulgate, which is not strictly in accordance with the Greek, though sufficiently so for my present purpose. He also prints " This is my blood," in capitals, and the explanatory words, " of the New Testament," in ordinary type, thus: "THIS IS MY BLOOD of the New Testament."

forms of consecration,—' This *is* my body, This *is* my blood.' . . . It is impossible for me, by any commentary or paraphrase I can make, to render our Saviour's words more explicit, or reduce them to a form more completely expressing the Catholic doctrine than they do themselves. The Catholic doctrine teaches that it *was* Christ's body, and that it *was* His blood" (Lect. xv., p. 174).

Now it is evident that had Cardinal Wiseman selected his text from Luke, instead of from Matthew, he would have had no pretence for his argument. For according to Luke, the Lord did not say, *simpliciter*, "This is my body," but "This is my body, which is given for you," viz., His crucified body; and He adds, "This do in remembrance of me," thereby showing that the Lord was instituting a commemorative ceremony. Neither does He say, "This is my blood," nor any words to that effect, but, on the contrary, He expressly says, "This is the *New Testament in my blood.*"

Hence it follows that, assuming we are bound by the literal interpretation, and that the Lord was referring to the bread and wine, and also assuming that the text of Matthew (and the same may be said of Mark), if it stood alone, would bear the interpretation contended for by Cardinal Wiseman,—according to Luke, also literally interpreted, the bread and wine were merely symbols—the one of Christ's cruci-

fied body, and the other (not of His blood, but) of the
New Testament in His blood.

The question therefore naturally arises, which of
the two accounts is the correct one? As they at
present stand, there is no sufficient reason for pre-
ferring the one to the others, and nevertheless the
one, as interpreted by Roman Catholics, leads to a
totally different meaning from the other, as interpreted
both by Protestants and by Roman Catholics. So
that, had we nothing but the gospel accounts to rely
upon, we should be in the position so graphically
described by Cardinal Wiseman in his sixteenth
lecture.

" Can any of you," he says, " conceive yourselves,
if, with a certain prophetic assurance that in a few
more hours you would be taken away from your
family and friends, you had called them around you,
to make to them your last bequests, and explained
what you wished to be performed in remembrance of
you for ever, that which was more especially to bind
them after your death to your memory,—can you
imagine yourselves making use of words, of their very
nature, leading to a totally different meaning from
what you had in your mind, or wished to appoint?
And suppose that you were gifted with a still greater
degree of foresight, and could see what would in
future be the result of using these words,—how by
far the greater part of your children, not believing it

possible that you could have had any hidden meaning on such an occasion, would determine to take your words quite literally, whence you foresaw the complete defeat or perversion of your wishes, while only a very small number would divine that you had spoken figuratively,—do you thing that under such circumstances you would choose that phraseology, when it was possible, without the waste of another syllable, explicitly to state the true meaning which you wished them to receive?" (Lect. xvi., p. 213). No words can more accurately define the position in which we should have been left had we been limited to the gospel narratives. But to complete the analogy, we must further suppose, that after they had received your instructions, your relations had retired into an adjoining room, and that three of them had committed to writing what they imagined you had told them; but that, on comparing their several accounts, there were found to be certain verbal disagreements tending to different inferences, and that some doubt had arisen, or might possibly arise, as to which of them was the correct one : would you not, humanly speaking, so soon as you were informed of what had happened, if you still retained sufficient strength, have availed yourself of the opportunity to prevent any such misunderstanding, by repeating what you had really said? Now this is precisely what the Lord in His infinite condescension has done. For we are

informed that He subsequently instructed His chosen
apostle Paul as to the actual words He had used.
So that from thenceforth we have a perfect standard
of truth in the Epistles of Paul, whereby to correct
any apparent discrepancies in the Gospels.

But before quitting the Evangelists, it may be as
well to add a few words on what they report the Lord
to have said.

The language of Christ, as recorded by Matthew
and Mark, was, according to our authorised version, " This is my body,"—a form of expression
which, if taken in its strictest literal and primary sense, without any explanatory or additional
words, would amount to, that the THIS (to whatever it may have referred) was identical with His
then existing body as present to the apostles. On
the other hand, Luke tells us that He was alluding
to His CRUCIFIED BODY; "This is my body which is
given for you." All the accounts agree in that He
spoke figuratively of the wine. The words attributed
to Him by each of them are to the same purport, viz.,
that He described the wine under the symbol of "*the
cup*" which contained it. They are also further
agreed, that in speaking of the wine, He did not
(*simpliciter*) say, "This is my blood," as quoted by
Cardinal Wiseman, but "This is my blood of the
New Testament," as in Matthew and Mark; or, according to Luke, "This cup is the New Testament

in my blood;" each form of expression evidently
meaning the same thing, viz., His testament confirmed or sealed in His blood.

It still remains to ascertain whether He be correctly
represented in our authorised version of Matthew and
Mark, who imputed to Him the words, " THIS IS MY
BODY." Did He ever, in fact, make use of that form
of expression? If He did, it would still be open to
inquiry, what He meant by it. But if He did not,
then the entire argument of Cardinal Wiseman and
his modern ritualistic admirers falls to the ground.

The Roman Catholic views are thus concisely and
exhaustively put by Cardinal Wiseman: " It is evident that the words (This is my body), simply considered,—if there were no question about any apparent
impossibility, and if they related to some other matter,
—would be at once literally believed by any one who
believes at all in the words of Christ. His reasoning
would naturally be, ' Christ has declared this doctrine
in the simplest terms, and I receive it on His word.'
There must be a reason, as I shall fully prove to you
just now, for departing in this case from the ordinary,
simple interpretation of the words, and giving them
a tropical meaning. It is for them who say that
Christ, by the words, ' This is my body,' meant no
more than, ' This is the figure of my body,' to give us
a reason why their interpretation is correct. The
words themselves express that it is the body of

Christ" (Lect. xv., p. 174). Such is the argument of
the Roman Catholics, as propounded by Cardinal
Wiseman ; and the ingenuity of man could not add to
its force were volumes to be written upon it. The
case, in fact, is in a nutshell, viz., that the words of
Christ were, "This *is* my body," whatever be intended by the demonstrative pronoun "THIS." The
answer is fortunately equally simple, namely, that He
did not say, "This *is* my body." Such may have
been His meaning, but He did not so express Himself.

Now, what were the actual facts of the case?
According to Cardinal Wiseman—and the same is
held by other competent authorities—the language
spoken by our Saviour was Aramaic (see Lect. xiv.,
p. 152); and in the Aramaic the verb "to be" is
never employed in the present tense. If the reader
will do me the favour of referring to the Appendix,
he will find that, "In the Semitic languages the
present tense of the verb ' to be,' which, in the Arian
languages, forms the copula between the subject and
the predicate of a preposition, *cannot* appear, because
the Semitic languages have not what we call the
present tense of a verb ; " and further, that "From
the grammatical form itself of the formula, ' *This is
my body*,' as expressed in Syriac, or in any other
Semitic idiom, it is impossible to determine whether
the words have a literal or figurative meaning "
(Letter of Professor Marks, Nos. 6 and 7).

E

So also Dean Alford, who says, "On this much controverted word" (ἐστιν, is) "no stress is to be laid. In the original tongue, in which the Lord spoke, it would not be expressed; and, as it now stands, it is merely the logical copula between the subject, ' This,' and the predicate, ' my body'" (Alford's Gr. Test., Matt. xxvi. 26, note).

That, in Scripture phraseology, propositions precisely similar in form have frequently a secondary meaning, everybody admits; and the Protestant argument is, that the same form is equally applicable to indicate the relationship of identity and that of symbolism, and that consequently, from the mere form of expression, unexplained by its context, either interpretation would be equally possible.

Dr Adam Clarke, in his Commentary on the Bible, illustrates his argument by referring to a variety of texts where a similar form of expression is used. From among them, I content myself with the following, because, in respect to them, Cardinal Wiseman admits that the verb " to be " means *to represent*:— Gen. xli. 26, 27, " And the seven good kine *are* seven years." Dan. vii. 24, " The ten horns *are* ten kings." Matt. xiii. 38, 39, " The field *is* the world; the good seed *are* the children of the kingdom; the tares *are* the children of the wicked one; the enemy *is* the devil; the harvest *is* the end of the world; the reapers *are* the angels." 1 Cor. x. 4, " The rock *was* Christ." Gal. iv. 24, "For these *are* the two covenants." Rev. i. 20, "The seven stars *are* the angels of the seven churches." Nor is this form of expression peculiar to the Scriptures. There is no country or language in which the verb "to be" necessarily indicates the relationship of identity. It is almost, if not quite, as often employed to express that one thing represents another, for there is no figure of speech in more constant use than that of the ellipsis. Dr Adam Clarke mentions several instances by way of illustration; among others, where, in reference to a statue, we are told, "That *is* Cicero," "that *is* Cæsar." I remember being in a picture-gallery, where a friend, who happened to be with me at the time, called my attention to a landscape, and said, "That is one of Mr Evelyn's fields at Wotton;" by which I understood him to mean, "That is the picture of a field at Wotton, in the county of Surrey, the property of your nephew, Mr Evelyn." These instances are amply sufficient to show, that there is nothing forced or unnatural in interpreting the language of Christ, when He said, "This *is* my body" (assuming Him to have said so), to have meant, "This represents, or is a symbol of, my body."

Cardinal Wiseman is much pressed by the class of Scripture illustrations above selected from Dr Adam Clarke's Commentary on the Bible. He is obliged to admit that in them the verb "to be" means *to re-*

*present;* but he denies their applicability on the following grounds: namely, That they all relate to the interpretation of a vision, a parable, or a prophecy. He says, " When you tell me that ' This is my body' may mean ' This represents my body,' because in those passages the same verb or word occurs with this sense, I must, in like manner, ascertain, not only that the verb ' to be' is common to the text, but that the same thing is to be found in it as in them; in other words, that in the forms of institution, there was given the *explanation of some symbol,* such as the interpretation of a vision, a parable, or a prophecy. Show me this, as I can show it in all the others, then I will allow this to be parallel with them" (Lect. xv., p. 186). The italics are Cardinal Wiseman's; and what a sovereign contempt he must have entertained for the intellectual calibre of his audience when he emphasised those words ! For, though true it is, Christ was not interpreting a vision, a parable, or a prophecy, nothing can be more certain than that in the *forms* of institution there was given the explanation of some symbol. It may not, indeed, be so apparent in regard to the one form, viz., " This is my body." But what are we to say of the second ? " *This cup* is my blood of the New Testament," or " the New Testament in my blood." No person, I presume, will contend that Christ meant that *the cup* itself was either His blood or His testament.

He obviously intended the wine, as symbolised by the cup which contained it.

That the verb "to be" admits of the qualified interpretation contended for by Protestants in cases other than in the explanation of allegories, or dreams, or parables, is illustrated by the following forms of expression:—"I *am* the door" (John x. 7); "I *am* the true vine" (John xv. 1). These are, among a variety of other texts, relied upon by Dr Adam Clarke to prove that, in Scripture phraseology, the verb "to be" does not necessarily imply the relationship of identity. How does Cardinal Wiseman meet them? He does not pretend that they fall within the category of cases involving the explanation of an allegory, a dream, or a parable. But Dr Adam Clarke having interpreted them to mean, "I *represent* the door;" "I *represent* the true vine," Cardinal Wiseman takes issue upon the word "*to represent*," whether in fact Christ meant to say, "I *represent* the door;" "I *represent* the true vine." But let Cardinal Wiseman speak for himself.

"I ask any one," he says, "on reflection, to answer does 'to be,' in these passages, mean 'to *represent?*' Substitute the latter verb; for if the two be equivalent, the one must fit in the other's place. Compare them with the words, 'The Rock *was* Christ.' If you say, 'The Rock *represents* Christ,' the sense is the same, because 'to be,' is its equivalent, 'I *am* the door: I *represent* the door.'" To an ordinary mind, the sense would appear as unaltered as in the other case; but, continues Cardinal Wiseman, "that is not Christ's meaning." Now, what does the reader imagine to have been His meaning? "'I am *as* the door;' 'I *resemble* the door,' that is what He wished to express." So that by 'I am the door,' Christ did not mean, 'I *represent* the door,' but He meant to say, 'I *resemble* the door.'" It may be so for aught I know to the contrary; but, for the life of me, I cannot perceive any substantial difference between the two forms of expression. There is no magic in the word *to represent*. To *resemble* would have equally answered the conditions of the argument; nor is there any reason why Dr Adam Clarke should not have used it instead of the other. On referring to Webster's Dictionary, I find that "resemblance" is one of the synonyms for "representation," and "representation" one of the synonyms for "resemblance." So that, in either case, whichever word we use, the sense would remain substantially the same. Christ is obviously comparing Himself to a door and to a vine. His words, when translated from the Greek into English, were "I *am* the door," "I *am* the vine;"—a similar form of speech to that He is supposed to have used in reference to the bread, "This *is* my body." In the former cases, it is admitted that He did not mean to convey that He

was a real door or a real vine; but that, in some
sense or other, there was something analogous between Himself, in relation to His followers, and a
door or a vine. Dr Adam Clarke says His meaning
was, "I *represent* a door or a vine." No such thing,
says Cardinal Wiseman; He meant to say, "I *resemble* a door, or a vine." This nice distinction reminds one of the merry dispute among the Gypsies,
mentioned by honest Isaak Walton, where the point in
controversy was, whether it were easier to *rip* a cloak
or to *unrip* a cloak,—the two words in reality meaning
the same thing.

Cardinal Wiseman, in common with every Roman
Catholic controversialist with whose writings I
am at all acquainted, is in the constant habit
of misrepresenting his opponent's argument. One
would often imagine, from his way of putting it, that
Protestants argued as if the verb "to be" never
implied the relationship of identity. That is not the
case. What they contend for is, that the expression
"this *is* that," is a form of speech of doubtful significance, and that it is open to either interpretation,
viz., "this *represents* that," or "this is *identical*
with that;" and that, consequently, to ascertain the
sense in which it is used on any particular occasion,
we must take into consideration the attendant circumstances, and the entirety of what is said in connexion with it.

Take the following examples, as selected by Cardinal Wiseman:—

" The Word was God."

" The Rock was Christ."

" This is my body."

On comparing the several texts, Cardinal Wiseman says, " If in the third of these, we may change the verb, because we can do so in the second, what is to prevent our doing it in the first? and instead of the Word ' was God,' why not interpret, ' the Word represented God?' "

To which I answer:

If John had written nothing further bearing upon the subject than that " The Word was God," and were I strictly limited to those words, I could never be in a position to predicate with any degree of certainty in what sense he intended his words to be understood; for the words themselves, standing alone, would be capable of either interpretation, viz., that the Word was actually God, or that the Word represented God. But taking that particular text as interpreted by the entirety of what John wrote, and as compared with other texts of Scripture,* I infer that he intended to be understood as signifying the relationship of identity: and whether I be correct in so

---

* Mr Ainsley has noted a remarkable reading of John i. 18— "The only-begotten God," instead of Son. This reading occurs both in the Sinaitic and Vatican.

interpreting his words, the sense I impute to them is, at all events, not repugnant to his teaching taken as a whole, and therefore may have been his real meaning.

In like manner, had Christ merely said, " This is my body," and were there nothing explanatory in the circumstances of the case, those words, standing simply and alone, would not have afforded the means of ascertaining with certainty what it was that He intended us to understand by them : inasmuch as, consistently with the conventional forms of speech, they might with equal propriety be construed either way, viz., that the " THIS " was identical with His body, or that it represented His body. But if taken in connexion with the surrounding circumstances, with the entirety of what the Lord said on the same occasion, and with the explanation subsequently given by Paul, they can only bear the one interpretation, viz., that it represented His body ; for to interpret them as meaning the relationship of identity, would neutralise and make insensible all that subsequently followed : and we are confirmed in the propriety of this view by the fact that Cardinal Wiseman has never once, in the course of his argument, ventured to quote the entirety of what was said, or attempted to reconcile it with the construction he puts upon the verb " to be."

Thus far I have assumed, with Cardinal Wiseman

that the force of the sentence is dependent on the interpretation we give to the verb " to be." Whereas, in truth, as noticed by Dean Alford, the verb " to be" is only the logical copula between the subject and the predicate. The force of the sentence is dependent on the meaning we attach to the demonstrative pronoun " THIS," as will be at once apparent on reference being had to the text. Take the words as quoted by Cardinal Wiseman. " We have here," he says, " two forms of consecration, ' This is my body ;' ' This is my blood.'" Let us confine ourselves to the first of the above forms, the second is obviously an imperfect quotation of the language of the Lord.

" This is my body." What did Christ intend to convey by the demonstrative pronoun " THIS ? " If, as Cardinal Wiseman would have us infer, the Lord was alluding to the bread, then the words would be equivalent to, " This *bread* is my body ;" and, in such case, those who believe in the doctrine of transubstantiation might, with some show of plausibility, urge that the language of the Lord was at all events susceptible of the meaning they attach to it. But if, on the other hand, the demonstrative pronoun " THIS " did not and could not have referred to the *bread*, then it would not be true that Christ had declared the bread to be His body, no matter what significance we assign to the verb " to be;" and, consequently,

all those who believe in the doctrine of transubstantiation, because they imagine Christ to have so
expressed Himself, and that they have Scripture
warrant for the faith they profess, would be simply
deceiving themselves. Their worship of the host
will, according to Cardinal Fisher, have been an act
of gross idolatry, in that they will have adored the
creature, bread, instead of the Creator.

The force of the demonstrative pronoun does not
fully present itself in our English version; because,
in English, it is not declinable, and has no genders,
the same word being equally applicable to nouns of
every gender, masculine, feminine, and neuter. But it
is otherwise in Greek, and we must therefore have
resort to what the Evangelists wrote or sanctioned in
Greek, in order to ascertain the force and meaning
of their expressions, as understood by themselves and
adopted by the apostles. In passing, however, I
would observe, that it is difficult to reconcile even the
English version with Cardinal Wiseman's views.
According to our authorised version, we read, in 1
Cor. xi. 23, 24, "That the Lord Jesus, the same
night that He was betrayed, took bread: and when
He had given thanks, He brake it, and said, Take,
eat: this is my body, which is broken for you: this
do in remembrance of me."

From the above it is obvious that the demonstrative pronoun is repeated, and that in each occasion

it refers to the same noun-substantive,—" THIS is
my body; THIS do in remembrance of me." But
how is it possible that the noun should be BREAD?
Try it. Make the experiment by completing the
sentence, and the absurdity will be apparent. " This
bread is my body; this bread do in remembrance of me."
How could the Lord be supposed to have said, " This
bread *do* in remembrance of me?" He might,
indeed, have said, " This bread *is* my body;" but
" This bread *do*," is nonsense. Hence, the noun-
substantive could not have been BREAD, whatever
else it may have been.

But any obscurity there may be in interpreting
the English version is instantly dissipated when we
turn to the text as we have it in Greek. However
the several accounts may differ in other respects,
they all agree in rendering the demonstrative pronoun " this" by τοῦτο, thus : τοῦτό ἐστιν τὸ σῶμά
μου, *i.e.*, by a demonstrative pronoun of the *neuter
gender*, and which, therefore, could not refer to
ἄρτος, bread, which is a noun of the *masculine
gender*. This peculiarity of expression is so absolutely conclusive on the question at issue, that
I am surprised it has not been noticed by earlier
controversial writers. So far as I am aware, the
learned Dean Alford was the first to call attention
to it in a note to his Greek Testament, where he
says, " τοῦτό ἐστιν τὸ σῶμά μου. τοῦτο, this which

I now offer to you, this *bread*. The form of expression is important, not being οὗτος ὁ ἄρτος, or οὗτος ὁ οἶνος, but τοῦτο in both cases, or τοῦτο τὸ ποτήριον, not the bread or wine itself, but the *thing* in each case, precluding all idea of a substantial change" (Alford's Gr. Test., Matt. xxvi. 26, note).

I confess there appears to me a little obscurity in Dean Alford's commentary on this remarkable passage. It is not sufficiently obvious what he intended to convey by "the *thing* in each case." This much I clearly understand, that it cannot mean the bread; for, in that case, the pronoun would have been οὗτος, not τοῦτο: τοῦτο cannot by any rule of grammatical construction be made to agree with ἄρτος. To whatever it refers, its noun, whether expressed or understood, must have been *a noun of the neuter gender, indicative of action.* Let us examine the matter a little more closely, and possibly we may arrive at a definite solution.

All the ceremonial law was more or less typical of the Messiah that was to come; but there was no ceremony so plenarily significative of Him as the feast of the Passover. "For even Christ *our Passover* is sacrificed for us" (1 Cor. v. 7).

The two principal features of the feast of the Passover were a lamb and unleavened bread. The lamb—which was to be without blemish, a male of the first year—was to be slain and its blood to be shed, but the Israelites were strictly enjoined not to " break a bone thereof" (Exod. xii. 46). Together with the lamb, they were also to eat unleavened bread. The *lamb* without blemish typified the spotless purity of the Lord's life; the *unleavened bread,* corresponded to His body, which was to be characterised by this peculiarity, that it was not to see corruption (Ps. xvi. 10; Acts ii. 27, and xiii. 35). The greatest stress was consequently laid upon the absence of leaven, which consists of dough in a state of fermentation or incipient decomposition. To preclude the possibility of any accidental mixture of the slightest particle of leaven, it was commanded, under the severest penalties, that " Seven days shall there be no leaven found in your houses: for whoever eateth that which is leavened, even that soul shall be cut off from the congregation of Israel, whether he be a stranger or born in the land" (Exod. xii. 19). Hence, in estimating the force of the language of institution, the reader should bear in mind that UN-LEAVENED BREAD had always been symbolical of Christ's body.

We now turn to what occurred on the memorable occasion of the Last Supper; and that there may be no question or dispute as to the correct interpretation of what fell from Christ, I shall confine myself to the account as handed down to us by Paul. My reasons are sufficiently obvious.

Matthew originally wrote his Gospel in Hebrew, or probably Aramaic, and the learned are not agreed by whom the translation into Greek was made. Some imagine that Matthew first wrote in Hebrew, and that his book was afterward rewritten in Greek by himself; others, that it was translated under apostolic authority. The former is Olshausen's view, the latter Mayer's. (See introductory remarks to the Gospel according to Matthew in the Critical English Testament.) Similar doubts have been suggested in regard to the Gospel of Mark: some contending that Mark originally wrote in Latin; others, that he wrote in Greek. In the Peschito we read, "Finished is the Holy Gospel, the preaching of Markos; which he spake and preached in Roman at Rumi" (Peschito, by Etheridge). On the other hand, Tregelles maintains that Mark wrote in Greek, and says that the subscriptions to the several Gospels in the Peschito are of no authority whatever. (See Horne's Introduction, by Tregelles, vol. iv., 437, 12th edition, where the authorities on the subject are referred to.) All are agreed that Luke wrote in Greek; but he was not present when the words were spoken, and in some particulars he differs from Matthew, who was present. But in respect to the First Corinthians there is no important difference of opinion that I am aware of. Indeed, its authenticity is even admitted by infidel writers. The text I shall adopt for the English is that of our authorised version, edited by Tischendorf, and for the Greek Ἡ καινὴ Διαθήκη, Griesbach's text, with the various readings of Mill and Scholz, 4th edition, 1868. " For I received of the Lord, what also I delivered unto you, That the Lord Jesus in the night in which He was betrayed took bread (ἄρτον, masculine): And having given thanks, He broke and said, Take, eat: This (τοῦτο, the neuter of οὗτος) is my body which is for you broken: * This (τοῦτο) do in remembrance (ἀνάμνησιν) of me. In like manner also the cup, when He had supped, saying, This cup is the New Testament in my blood: This (τοῦτο) do ye, as oft as ye drink, in remembrance (ἀνάμνησιν) of me.

The Lord, at the time of which we are speaking, was celebrating the feast of the Passover, and consequently the bread was the UNLEAVENED BREAD used on such occasions. It is also to be observed, that the Lord does not mention bread; that is to say, He does not utter the word ἄρτος, bread. What actually occurred was, that He took a piece of the PASCHAL

---

* The Sinaitic, Vatican, and Alexandrian omit the word "*broken*." But some such word is necessary to complete the sentence, which, as it stands in the Sinaitic, Vatican, and Alexandrian, is clearly imperfect. In the corresponding passage in Luke xxii. 19, they supply the omission by the word "*given*,"— "*which is given for you.*" Griesbach, Mill, and Scholz adopt the same form in Luke xxii. 19. But in 1 Cor. xi. 24, instead of διδόμενον (given), they read, as in our authorised version, κλώμενον (broken), and the Peschito agrees with them in both readings.

UNLEAVENED BREAD into His hand, and having given
thanks, He brake and said, "This" (that which
He held in His hand, or the fragments of the
BROKEN PASCHAL UNLEAVENED BREAD) "is my body,
which for you is BROKEN." That the Lord did not
intend to be understood as referring to the bread as
bread, follows from the fact that in that case the demonstrative pronoun, THIS, would in Greek have been
οὗτος, whereas it is τοῦτο, and of necessity, therefore,
can only refer to some noun of the neuter gender.
The noun itself is not expressed, and therefore we
may reasonably presume that, from the attendant circumstances, it was a word that would naturally suggest itself to the audience.

But what were the attendant circumstances?
Why, that the Lord held in His hand a piece of the
PASCHAL UNLEAVENED BREAD, which, assuming Him
to be the promised Messiah, as all His disciples believed Him to be, was notoriously a *symbol* significative of His body, and which, therefore, on being
*broken*, became a symbol of the death He was to die.
Now the word that answers the conditions of the
problem, and gives effect to the entirety of what fell
from the Lord is, not ἄρτος, bread, but πρᾶγμα, an
act; and on introducing this word, the text would
read, "τοῦτο τὸ πρᾶγμά μου ἐστὶ τὸ σῶμα τὸ ὑπὲρ
ὑμῶν κλώμενον." "This act" (namely, of breaking the
bread) "is my body, which for you is broken:" that

F

is to say, was symbolic of the breaking of His body
on the cross.

Immediately following the above, the Lord adds,
" This do in remembrance of me." The word here
rendered by " remembrance," in the Greek is ἀνάμνησιν, and strictly means a remembrance in the
nature of a memorial. Parkhurst says that Scholz
seems always to translate the word as *memorial*, and
that the proper rendering of the passage is, " for a
memorial or remembrance of me." (See Parkhurst,
5th edit.) In the Epistle to the Hebrews, the same
word is applied to the symbolic sacrifices under the
old law. " But in these (sacrifices) there is a remembrance (ἀνάμνησις) again for sins every year'
(Heb. x. 3). That the wine is spoken of symbolically is apparent on the face of the text. The Lord
did not say, as represented by Cardinal Wiseman,
" This is my blood," but " This cup is the New Testament in my blood ;" and thereupon He added a
precisely similar form of injunction to that which He
had delivered in respect to the bread: " This do ye,
as oft as ye drink, in remembrance (ἀνάμνησιν) of
me."

From the above it follows, that if there be any
intelligible meaning in words, the Lord could only
have spoken of the BROKEN BREAD and the CUP
as symbols of what was about to happen : because, in
the first place, that to which He assimilates them had

no existence at the time—His body had not then
been broken, nor had His blood been shed; and,
secondly, because He speaks of them as MEMORIALS,
which precludes the idea of identity. A man cannot be a memorial of himself. The very expression
implies something to recall to mind somebody or
something else that is absent.

To the same effect is Paul's commentary on the
words of institution: "For as often as ye eat this
bread, and drink the cup, ye do show forth the
Lord's death till He come."

"Ye do show forth." The word we here translate "show forth," in the Greek is καταγγέλλετε, and
literally means to proclaim or commemorate. (See
Parkhurst, 5th edit.; and see further, on the force
of καταγγέλλετε, an article in The Rock, June 25,
1869, by Daniel Bagot, Dean of Dromore.) And
what was it we were ordered to proclaim or commemorate? The Lord's DEATH, not His PRESENCE.
This it is that we are commanded to commemorate
"till He come." But it would be sheer nonsense,
unintelligible jargon, to direct us to commemorate
the Lord's death till He come, if, in the very act of
commemoration, He were then and there bodily
present.

I cannot help suspecting that Protestant writers
would have written to greater effect had they paid
more attention to the force of the expressions they

are in the habit of using. They generally start with
the erroneous notion that when Christ said, "This is
my body," He was referring to the bread; and seeing
how improbable it was that Christ should have intended that the bread He held in His hand was
actually His body, they explain His words as though
they had been, "This represents or is symbolic of
my body;" and unfortunately they justify the substituting of one form of expression for its equivalent
by representing Christ as having spoken in *figurative
language*, without defining the class of figurative
speech to which they allude. Thereupon Cardinal
Wiseman, skilfully introducing *tropical* for *figurative*,
challenges them to adduce any sufficient reason for
departing from the ordinary simple interpretation of
the words and giving them a *tropical meaning*.
(Lect. xv., p. 174.) Nor am I prepared to say that
Cardinal Wiseman has in this exceeded the daily
practice of professional advocacy. A moment's reflection will, however, suffice to expose the fallacy.

A *trope* in rhetoric is a word or expression used
in a different sense from that which it properly
signifies, or a word changed from its original signification to another for the sake of giving life or
emphasis to an idea,—as when we call a shrewd
man a fox. (See Webster's Dictionary.) In this
sense there was nothing figurative in what Christ
said.

The only figure of speech made use of by the Lord was that called the *ellipsis*, which is to ordinary language what stenography is to ordinary writing, and admits of the most literal interpretation. Webster defines an ellipsis in grammar to be "a defect, an omission, a figure of syntax by which one or more words are omitted." For example, when my friend already alluded to said to me, "That is one of Mr Evelyn's fields at Wotton," there was nothing tropical in his words,—they were merely elliptical. He meant me *literally* to understand what his words, if amplified, would have literally expressed. So also when the Lord, having broken a piece of the unleavened bread, distributed it among His disciples, and said, "This is my body, which is broken for you," He was evidently speaking elliptically; for He does not mention to what "*this*" referred. To the full development of the sentiment, we must amplify what was said by introducing one or more other word or words, whether bread or something else. I have shown that the word or words so omitted could not have been bread, for in that case the demonstrative pronoun would have been οὗτος instead of τοῦτο; and I have also shown that He was speaking of some *action* on His part, inasmuch as He tells them to do the same thing as He had done: " This *do* in remembrance of me."

Taking all the above circumstances into consideration, and bearing in mind that the Lord, though not speaking tropically, was expressing Himself elliptically, I would venture to suggest the following as correctly representing *what He was understood by the Evangelist and the apostles to have intended to convey.*

The Lord, we are told, took of the Paschal unleavened bread, and having given thanks to the Almighty, broke the bread and distributed it among those who were present, saying, "Take, eat; this that I have done" (namely, the breaking of the bread) "is symbolic of my body broken for you; this *do*" (namely, that which you have seen me do) "in remembrance of me." After the same manner, also, the cup, when He had supped, saying, "The contents of this cup is symbolic of the New Testament, confirmed by the shedding of my blood: this do ye" (namely, distribute wine among yourselves) "in remembrance of me."

What remains of the fifteenth lecture is principally devoted to controverting a corroboratory argument suggested by the late Dr Adam Clarke, and which only those who are sufficiently acquainted with the Hebrew and Aramaic languages are competent to deal with. Being myself among the incompetent, I submitted a case for the opinion of a learned Hebrew professor of one of the universities, who, with that kindness and condescension that are characteristic of him, favoured me with a full and impartial answer. The reader will find it in the Appendix.

I cannot conclude my remarks on this fifteenth lecture without again directing attention to the two leading misconceptions on the part of Cardinal Wiseman, and which pervade the whole of his argument. He all along assumes that the demonstrative pronoun, THIS, is referable to the bread and wine, whereas I have endeavoured, and I trust successfully, to prove that it could only have referred to something Christ was *doing* at the time, namely, to the breaking of the bread and the distributing of the wine. Then, again, he erroneously assumes that Protestants have no other reason for interpreting the verb "to be" to signify "to symbolise" or "to represent," than that in some other instances it will bear that meaning. There cannot be a more mistaken view of the case. Protestants readily assent to the proposition that, as a general rule, words should be interpreted in their primary sense. It is only when, from the attendant circumstances and the accompanying words, the meaning of the sentence necessitates a different construction, that they have resort to a secondary sense. To justify a secondary sense they are driven to the necessity of comparing the text in question with other analogous forms of expression, and the further they pursue their inquiries, the more apparent it becomes that the verb "to be" is almost as constantly "used" to indicate the relation of symbolism as that of identity. I myself do not feel the necessity of substituting "represents" for "is." It appears to me that Christ was expressing Himself elliptically, and I read His words, "This" (namely, the breaking of the bread) "*is* the symbol of my body broken for you." But there is nothing forced in the other form of expression,—"This represents my body," the meaning being substantially the same in both cases.

So natural is it to speak of the symbol as the thing signified, that we often imperceptibly have resort to that form of speech; of which, indeed, the words of institution afford an apt illustration: "This cup is the New Testament in my blood," obviously meaning, not the cup, but the wine. But so easy is the transition of thought, that few people (not even apparently Cardinal Wiseman himself) are aware that no mention is made of the wine as wine. It is always spoken of as "the cup," or as "the fruit of the vine."

Had Cardinal Wiseman felt himself competent to grapple with the question on its merits, he would not have laboured so hard on the various texts which had been referred to merely as matter of illustration, but would at once have addressed himself to the main question in dispute, namely, whether, consistently with all we read, the language of institution be capable of an intelligible meaning, if construed as he has contended for. This, however, he has altogether evaded ; and, instead thereof, has, with such consummate skill, diverted attention from essentials to matters comparatively immaterial, that many of his readers imagine he has most satisfactorily proved what he has not even attempted.

# CHAPTER II.

CARDINAL WISEMAN's argument on the subject of transubstantiation concludes with his sixteenth lecture, which is supplementary to the other two. It commences, after a few introductory remarks, with a lengthened and well-sustained argument in answer to those who object to his doctrine on the ground of its internal impossibility. But as I have not raised that objection, but have been content to meet Cardinal Wiseman upon his own grounds, and have even accepted his own tests of interpretation, it will be unnecessary to trouble either my readers or myself with any remarks upon that portion of the lecture. That there may be no misunderstanding in respect to the point in issue, it may be as well to state, that, throughout my answer, I have assumed the doctrine of transubstantiation to fall within the category of miracles, and that the only matter in dispute between us is simply a question of interpretation, viz., what was the meaning intended to be conveyed by the Lord in the words of institution ? This being premised, I proceed to the consideration of the confirmatory arguments adduced by Cardinal Wiseman, commencing at about the middle of page 212.

Cardinal Wiseman sums up the result of his argument, in answer to those who reject the doctrine, as involving a physical impossibility, in the following words:—" Thus it would appear, that the ground " (as if that were the only ground) " on which it is maintained that we must depart from the literal sense, is untenable,—untenable on philosophical grounds, as well as on principles of biblical interpretation." " But," he adds, " besides this mere rejection of the motives whereon the literal sense is abandoned, we have ourselves strong and positive confirmation of it."

The first of these confirmatory circumstances turns upon the grammatical construction of the words themselves, in which he says, the pronoun τοῦτο is put in a vague form. This being purely a matter of verbal criticism, I have nothing to add to what I have already said. The reader must take upon himself the trouble of comparing the opposing views of Dean Alford in his edition of the Greek Testament (note, in loc.), and Cardinal Wiseman ; and of making his election between them. But lest he should not have a copy of the lectures at hand, I will quote the passage in extenso.

" The very words themselves in which the pronoun is put in a vague form, strongly uphold us. Had our Saviour said, ' This bread is my body,—this wine is my blood,' there would have been some contradiction,—the apostles might have said, ' Wine cannot be His blood,—bread cannot be a body;' but when our Saviour uses this indefinite word, we arrive at its meaning only at the conclusion of the sentence, by that which is predicated of it. When we find in Greek there is a discrepancy of gender between that pronoun and the word ' bread,' it is more evident that He wished to define the pronoun, and give it its character, as designating His body and blood; so that by analysing the words themselves, they give us our meaning positively and essentially."

The reader must make what he can of the above. It seems to me to amount to nothing more nor less than an absolute and unqualified abandonment of the case. What Cardinal Wiseman had undertaken to prove was, that that which had originally been bread and wine, by force of the words of consecration, ceased to be bread and wine, and was transmuted into the substantial body and blood of Christ. And his proof consisted in the fact that the Lord had so stated it in words so clear,—" This *is* my body—this *is* my blood,"—that no paraphrase or commentary on his part could make it clearer. But now he tells us that the apostles did not understand Him to have said that the bread was His body, and the wine His blood ; and that he used the pronoun in a gender different from that of bread expressly that He might not have been so interpreted ; for that if He had said, " This bread is my body—this wine is my blood," there would have been some contradiction, and the apostles would have said, " Wine cannot be His blood —bread cannot be a body ; " but that when we find in Greek there is a discrepancy of gender between the pronoun and the word " bread," it is more evident that He wished to define the pronoun and give it its character as designating His body and blood. But, that the pronoun referred to His body and blood never was nor could have been disputed. For the one is the subject and the other the predicate of the sentence. What Cardinal Wiseman had undertaken to prove was, not that that which the neuter pronoun represented was Christ's body, but that the bread was. Whereas it now appears that the Lord had carefully guarded Himself against being so understood, for that His apostles would have rejected such a doctrine as involving an impossibility.

For the convenience of the reader, I will place the following extracts from these celebrated lectures in juxtaposition. He should compare those in the one column with that in the other :—

" In the Blessed Eucharist, that which was originally bread and wine is, by consecration, changed into the substance of the body and blood of our Lord, together with His soul and divinity ;

"Had our Saviour said, 'This bread is my body, —this wine is my blood,' there would have been some contradiction. The apostles might have said, ' Wine cannot be His blood ; bread can-in other words, His complete and entire person, as defined by the Council of Trent" (Lect. xiv., p. 136).

" We have here two forms of consecration, ' This *is* my body—this is my blood.' . . . It is impossible for me, by any commentary or para. phrase I can make, to render our Saviour's words more ex-plicit, or reduce them to a form more completely ex-pressing the Catholic doctrine than they do themselves " (Lect. xv., p. 174).

not be a body'" (Lect. xvi., p. 212).

The second confirmatory circumstance arises from the words of institution, " This is my body, which is broken, or delivered, for you ; and this is my blood, which is shed." Passing over the obvious objection, that the words as quoted are not those of the text, I have nothing to complain of in respect to the in-ference Cardinal Wiseman deduces from them. The only commentary he makes is as follows :—" By the addition of these adjuncts to the thing, by uniting to them what could only be said of His true body and blood, it would appear that He wanted still more to define and identify the object which He signified." This is actually all that Cardinal Wiseman says upon the subject! He does not attempt to reconcile the additional words with his theory of transubstantiation, or to explain *what* the object was which Christ signified and wanted still more to define and identify. In his exposition, as he leaves it, I entirely concur. It is, in truth, precisely what I have all along contended for. No Protestant, that I am aware of, doubts but that what the Lord said of His body and His blood had reference to His natural body and blood. But what we contend is, that He did not mean to imply any change in the substance of the bread and wine, for that the additional words were inconsistent with such an idea, and conclusively show that it was not to His body in its then state that He assimilated the bread, but to His crucified body, His body broken for us on the cross.

Cardinal Wiseman having thus summarily, but unsuccessfully, disposed of the first two corroboratory points, proceeds to the consideration of the third,* arising from the circumstances in which our blessed Saviour was placed. For this purpose, he imagines a person on his deathbed desirous of instituting a ceremony, to be thereafter observed by his relatives, in remembrance of him; and he asks, in substance, whether such a one would not have been anxious so to express himself as that his meaning should be free from ambiguity. No doubt he would; and that is precisely what the Lord has done. Humanly

---

* The third and fourth points are substantially involved in each other, and constitute only one.

speaking, He could not have conveyed His meaning more clearly. In order to create a difficulty, it is necessary to misquote His language. His words, taken in their integrity, are free from doubt. Let us see what they were, not confining ourselves to any one account, but taking them all collectively. The Lord Jesus, being at supper with His disciples, whilst they were eating, took apparently of the bread that was on the table, and after He had given thanks, brake and gave to His disciples, and said, "Take, eat; this (τοῦτο) is my body, which is given for you. This (τοῦτο) do in remembrance, or as a memorial of me. And in the same manner also the cup, when He had supped, saying, Drink ye all of it; this cup is the New Testament in my blood, or my blood of the New Testament, which is shed for many, for the remission of sins. This (τοῦτο) do as oft as ye drink, in remembrance, or as a memorial, of me. But I say unto you, that I will not drink henceforth of the fruit of the vine, until that day when I drink it new with you in my Father's kingdom." And Paul adds by way of explanation, "For as often as ye eat this bread and drink this cup, ye do" (καταγγέλλετε, see Parkhurst, ed. 1841) "commemorate the Lord's death till He come." There is no ambiguity in the above. On the contrary, His meaning is so obvious, that to enable Cardinal Wiseman to adapt it to his theory, he was necessitated to substitute other words in their stead, and thus to make it appear that Christ had said the very reverse of what He did say.

I now proceed to the consideration of the two remaining passages of Scripture referrred to by Cardinal Wiseman as corroboratory of his theory.

The first is from 1 Corinthians x. 16, where Paul says, " The cup of blessing which we bless, is it not the communion, or participation (κοινωνία), of the blood of Christ? and the bread which we break, is it not the communion, or participation (κοινωνία), of the body of Christ?" (For the force of the word κοινωνία, see Parkhurst, ed. 1841.)

It is to be observed that Paul does not here say that the sacramental cup *is* the blood of Christ; or the bread, His body: but that those who drink the one and eat the other participate in His blood and body. This is precisely what is held by the Anglican Church, and hence it is that that portion of its liturgy set apart for the administration of the Lord's Supper is called the " Communion Service."

But let us examine the text a little more closely.

Paul is not merely contrasting the Jewish and heathenish rites with those of the Christians, as Cardinal Wiseman has it, but is warning the Corinthians against the practices of idolatry, and illustrating by means of the Lord's Supper wherein the sin of sacrificial worship consists. He begins with, " Wherefore, my dearly beloved, flee from idolatry.

G

I speak as to wise men; judge ye what I say."
Having thus introduced the subject, he puts it to
them interrogatively, "The cup of blessing which
we bless, is it not the participation (on our part) of
the blood of Christ? The bread which we break,
is it not the participation (on our part) of the body of
Christ? For," he continues, "we being many, are
one bread, one body: for we are all partakers of that
one bread." That is to say, from the act of drinking
the wine and eating the bread that is consecrated to
Christ, we spiritually participate in the worship of
Him. Similarly he says, "Behold Israel after the
flesh. Are not they which eat of the sacrifices partakers of the altar?" meaning the worship of the
altar. "What say I then?" he continues; "that
the idol is anything? or that which is offered in
sacrifice to idols is anything? But that the things
which the Gentiles sacrifice, they sacrifice to devils,
and not to God: and I would not that ye should have
fellowship with devils. Ye cannot drink the cup of
the Lord, and the cup of devils: ye cannot be partakers of the Lord's table, and of the tables of devils."
His argument seems to be this: The idols are mere
blocks of wood and stone, and of themselves are
nothing more than any other pieces of wood or stone;
so also of the food sacrificed on the altar. It is the
same with the wine and bread, which, *per se*, are
nothing more than ordinary wine and unleavened

bread. But the efficacy of the latter arises from their being the emblems of a true worship, as that which constitutes the objection to the former arises from their being the emblems of idolatry. Apart from this latter consideration, it is immaterial whether we eat those things that have been sacrificed to idols or abstain from them; and therefore Paul adds, " Whatsoever is sold in the shambles, eat, asking no questions for conscience sake" (ver. 25). Hence, I agree with Cardinal Wiseman, that there exists a real contrast between the two cases. But, then, to make the contrast complete, the consecrated elements must correspond to the sacrificial victim. Both were really eaten, but as the victim was only emblematic of the object of worship, so the exigencies of the comparison would require that the bread and wine should only be emblematic of the body and blood of Christ.

I am happy to think that we have now arrived at the only remaining text referred to by Cardinal Wiseman, and I take the words as given by him: " He that eateth and drinketh unworthily, eateth and drinketh judgment to himself, not discerning the body of the Lord" (1 Cor. xi. 29). Again, " Whosoever shall eat this bread, or drink the chalice of the Lord unworthily, shall be *guilty of the body and blood of the Lord*" (1 Cor. xi. 27).

" What," says Cardinal Wiseman, " is the mean-

ing of discerning the body of Christ? Is it not to
distinguish it from ordinary food, to make a difference between it and other things? But if the body
of Christ be not really there, how can the offence be
considered as directed against the body of Christ?"
(Lect. xvi., p. 215). I must confess that if those
texts were independent texts and stood alone, they
might possibly admit of the construction contended
for. But Cardinal Wiseman has failed' to notice that
they were *inferences* from what had preceded them,
and are respectively introduced, the latter one (for
Cardinal Wiseman quotes them in an inverted order,
and omits to notice the intermediate or connecting
sentence) by " *Wherefore*," and the former by " *For*."
Hence, to arrive at their true meaning, we must compare them with what had been previously said.

It is to be collected from what Paul says, that the
Christian converts in Corinth had gradually come to
consider the Lord's Supper as an occasion for feasting
and revelry. In reproving them for this, he repeats
what he had previously told them relative to its
origin, namely, that it was instituted by the Lord
himself as a most solemn institution, to be thereafter
observed by His followers in remembrance of His
crucifixion. Hence He reminds them, that as often
as they eat the bread and drink the cup, they are
commemorating the Lord's death till He come.
" *Wherefore*," he adds, "whosoever shall eat this

bread and drink this cup unworthily" (that is to say, in the spirit of levity of which he is complaining) "shall be guilty of the body and blood of the Lord ;" or, in other words, shall be guilty of an offence against the body and blood of the Lord, by their contemptuous treatment of the ceremony He had directed to be observed in remembrance of them. And he therefore warns them to examine themselves before participating : "But let a man examine himself, and so let him eat of (that) bread and drink of (that) cup. FOR he that drinketh unworthily" (*i.e.,* in a spirit of levity), "eateth and drinketh his own damnation (or judgment to himself), "*not discerning the Lord's body :*" or, in other words, not regarding the solemnity of the occasion, or discerning that the bread and wine are emblematic of the Lord's body. Such, as it appears to me, is the true and only intelligible interpretation of the language of Paul when taken in its entirety.

The following case, that occurred on a trial for bigamy, at the Central Criminal Court, will afford an apt illustration of the texts in question :—

By the 9 Geo. IV., cap. 31, sec. 22, it is enacted, that, "If any person, being married, shall *marry* any other person during the life of the former husband or wife, . . . every such offender, and every one counselling, aiding, or abetting such offender, shall be guilty of felony."

Now it so happened that a married woman, leaving her husband, married the widower of her deceased sister ; and on their being prosecuted, the woman for bigamy, and the man for counselling her, it was contended on their behalf that the crime of bigamy could not be committed between a married woman and the widower of her sister, for that the 5 & 6 Will. IV., cap. 54, sec. 2, had enacted, that all marriages celebrated between persons so related should be " *absolutely null and void to all intents and purposes whatsoever.*" So that the supposed second marriage was, in fact, no marriage at all. It was a mere nullity, and could not have been anything else. But the court overruled the objection, and, the jury having found the prisoners guilty, sustained the conviction,—Lord Denman, Lord Chief-Justice, saying, " It is the appearing to contract a second marriage, and the going through the ceremony, that constitutes the crime of bigamy." (*R.* v. *Brown & Webb*, 1 C. and K., 144.) Similarly, the offence condemned by Paul was the pretending to participate in the sacrament of the body and blood of Christ, but doing it in such a tone of mind and spirit as converted into an insult to Almighty God what would otherwise have been acceptable to Him. This it is that Paul, to avoid circumlocution, intended to include under the form of expression, " Guilty of the BODY and BLOOD of CHRIST," and what he had previously declared in point of fact not to be a participating in the Lord's Supper at all. "This is not to eat the Lord's Supper" (1 Cor. xi. 20). In both cases, the acts complained of, so far as any advantage to be derived from them was concerned, were pronounced to be mere nullities. Strictly speaking, there was no second marriage, and there was no partaking of the Lord's Supper. But notwithstanding that, when contemplated from a criminal point of view, there was amply sufficient to constitute very grave offences —in the one case, an offence against the laws of England; in the other, an offence against the institutions of Christ.

It is a curious coincidence, that Cardinal Wiseman concludes the summing up of the various texts he had relied upon with illustrating the propriety of applying the conventional forms of speech in explanation of Scripture language. The instance he selects is the argument made use of by Protestants from the fact of the Lord still speaking of the "bread and wine" as bread and wine after the consecration of the elements. The text is not strictly correct as quoted by Cardinal Wiseman. Christ makes no mention of the bread after consecration, nor does He speak of the wine as *wine*, but calls it "*This* fruit of the vine," according to Matt. xxvi. 29. But for the moment I take the case as put by Cardinal Wiseman.

In answer to the supposed objection, Cardinal Wiseman refers to a variety of texts in proof of the fact that the use of these names after consecration is quite consistent with a change having taken place in the elements.

The man mentioned in the ninth chapter of John is spoken of as *the blind man* after he had been cured of his blindness (ver. 17). So in the case of Moses' rod, which is called *a rod* after it had been changed into a serpent. Similarly, the water is spoken of as *water* after it had been changed into wine. In justification of this form of speech, Cardinal Wiseman very properly refers to the recognised and conventional rules as applicable to all languages. " It is the usage," he says, " the common method of all language, when such a change occurs, to continue the original name " (Lect. xvi., p. 219). Cardinal Wiseman is strictly correct; nobody could doubt the propriety of the rule. But it ought to have occurred to him that the conventional usage of speech might have been applied with equal propriety to the interpretation of the otherwise ambiguous form of expression, " GUILTY OF THE BODY AND BLOOD OF CHRIST."

And here I would willingly close this portion of my case, were it not for the unfair statement of Cardinal Wiseman, to the effect that Protestants rely upon the circumstance of Christ having so spoken of the elements after consecration as their only resort in answer to the arguments, otherwise overwhelming, on the part of the Roman Catholics (p. 218). Whereas they only refer to it as matter incidental, as corroboratory of their interpretation of the words of institution, of which, in strictness, they formed no part, and are omitted by Luke and Paul. They were words graciously superadded by the Saviour, after the institution of the Lord's Supper was completed. Protestants rest their case on the language of institution itself. But as their interpretation of those words is disputed, they appeal with confidence, in corroboration of their views, to every other text directly or indirectly bearing on the subject.

But let not the Roman Catholic imagine that the superadded words fall within the category of illustrations above referred to by Cardinal Wiseman. There was something very remarkable in what fell from the Lord. The instances selected by Cardinal Wiseman are only additional examples of the use of that most common of all figures of speech called the ellipsis, where, to complete the sense, something has to be supplied by the audience. Thus, were one to speak of a man who had been cured of his blindness as *the blind man*, his audience would instinctively supply the omission, and understand him to mean *the man who had been blind*. So if, after consecration, Christ had said, " I will not drink of this cup," or even, " of this wine," it would have fallen within the rule. But He varies His form of expression, and does not speak of it as " this cup," or " this wine," but as " *this fruit of the vine*," as if He desired to preclude the idea of any change having taken place in regard to its substance.

Cardinal Wiseman concludes his sixteenth lecture with a reference to the writings of some of the early fathers of the third and following centuries. He says, " We naturally must desire, on a question of this kind, to ascertain the sentiments of antiquity" (p. 219); and I readily admit that there were individual authors of the third century who seem to have entertained the views for which Cardinal Wiseman contends. On the other hand, there were others who took a different view ; and it is a notorious fact that the Greek Church did not yield its assent to the doctrine earlier than A.D. 1672, though before then there might have been, and certainly were, individual churches in favour of it.

" I see plainly, and with my own eyes," says the incomparable Chillingworth, " that there are popes against popes, councils against councils, some fathers against other fathers, the same fathers against themselves, a consent of fathers of one age against a consent of fathers of another age, the church of one age against the church of another age " (" The Religion of Protestants," vi. 56). But were it otherwise, what can it matter what the early fathers thought, seeing that they professed to appeal to the same standard of truth as we ourselves do, and were only fallible men as we are? Assume that Cardinal Wiseman could have traced a belief in his doctrine up to the apostolic age, there would be no security against its being a false doctrine, inasmuch as we find that false doctrines were taught even in those early times, and we are emphatically warned that such would continue to be the case, more especially in the Church of Rome. For without discussing the question whether the Church of Rome be alluded to under the Antichrist of John, all antiquity concurs in applying to Rome what Paul says of the Man of Sin in his Second Epistle to the Thessalonians, chap. ii., where he tells us that "the mystery of iniquity doth already work," *i.e.*, even in his own days. Hence, were we able to trace the idea of the real presence to apostolic times, nevertheless, if it be not in accordance with Scripture, such a circumstance ought rather to operate as a caution against the reception of it, than as an argument in its favour. "To the law and to the testimony: if they speak not according to this word, it is because there is no light in them" (Isa. viii. 20).

But though, as is the case in the matters we have been considering, where the meaning and language of Holy Writ is so clear and explicit as not to admit of other than one consistent and rational interpretation, any declared opinion of the fathers at variance with apostolic teaching is entitled to no weight or consideration whatever; nevertheless, the patristic writings are not, on that account, to be cast aside as of little importance. To the church historian and to the biblical critic their value is absolutely beyond all price. They afford the most conclusive corroboratory evidence of the origin of Christianity as transmitted to us by the evangelists and by the apostles; they enable us to distinguish between spurious and authentic documents; and they materially assist the efforts that are being made to correct the textual errors of careless or designing transcribers : but in nothing are they of greater service than in operating as a wholesome warning against the ritualistic revivals of modern times, by the convincing proofs they have recorded of the gradual development of the unscriptural doctrines, the false traditions, the pious frauds, the episcopal pride, and the superstitious practices, that characterised and degraded the Primitive Church, even during the early ages of the second, third, and fourth centuries of our era.

I avail myself of the present opportunity to refer the reader to " Ancient Christianity," by the late Isaac Taylor; and to " Vigilantius and his Times," by Dr Gilly.

## NOTE ON 1 JOHN ii. 22.

It must not be inferred, from my not discussing a subject that is not essential to my argument, that I flinch from committing myself to an unpopular opinion, or that I entertain any serious doubts respecting it. Such is not the case. On the contrary, I am of opinion that Elliott has identified THE ANTICHRIST of John with THE MAN OF SIN of Paul to a very high degree of probability. (See "Horæ Apoc.," 5th edit. ; see also Elliott's review of Smith's "Bible Dictionary" in the *Christian Observer* for March 1864, and subsequently published separately.) I do not say that he has *conclusively* identified them, but that he has identified them to a very high degree of probability. I should not have hesitated to have used the stronger form of expression but for the doubtful authenticity of a portion of 1 John ii. 22.

We read in 1 John ii. 18 : " Ye have heard that Antichrist " (or the Antichrist) " shall come, even now there are many Antichrists." The above would seem to imply that at some future period would be developed he who was to be THE ANTICHRIST *par excellence ;* but that, in the meanwhile, he would partially appear under a variety of forms. In the text of Griesbach, he is described in the 18th verse as

" ὁ ἀντίχριστος," THE ANTICHRIST. Now, in the 22d and 23d verses of the same chapter, we read, " Who is a liar, but he that denieth that Jesus is the Christ? He is Antichrist, that denieth the FATHER AND THE SON. " Whosoever denieth the Son, the same hath not the Father; but he that acknowledgeth the Son, hath the Father also." Here also Griesbach has ὁ ἀντίχριστος, THE ANTICHRIST; as if John meant to identify him with THE ANTICHRIST, to whom he had previously alluded, and to distinguish him from other forms of Antichrist by this peculiarity, viz., that he would deny the FATHER AND THE SON. If this be the true reading, a question may fairly arise in its application to the Pope, whether this description be characteristic of the Church of Rome? whether, in fact, it can be truly predicated of the Church of Rome that she denies the FATHER AND THE SON in the sense intended by John? and it must be admitted that, if John did so express himself, the solution involves matter of considerable difficulty. I speak hypothetically, because the three most ancient manuscripts, the Sinaitic, Vatican, and Alexandrian, agree in the reading of our authorised version, and in the 22d verse omit the definite article. Consistently with them, the denying of the FATHER AND THE SON may have been only one of the many forms of Antichrist, and not necessarily indicative of THE ANTICHRIST, of whom John says, they had heard that he should come.

In a matter of so much controversial importance, and where the force of the text depends upon the insertion or omission of a single letter, the value of a reliable and independent authority is scarcely to be over-estimated. Fortunately such an authority has been preserved to us in the comparatively pure text of the venerable Peschito, where the corresponding passages read as follows:—

"As you have heard, THE FALSE MESHIHA cometh, and now there are many false Meshihas;" and again, "Who is a liar, if not he who denieth that Jeshu is the Meshiha? and this is A FALSE MESHIHA. He who denieth the Father, denieth also the Son; and he who denieth the Son, disbelieveth also the Father" ("Apostolic Acts and Epistles," by Etheridge, p. 423).

The Peschito, it will be observed, says nothing about denying the *Father and the Son*, as character-istic of THE FALSE MESHIHA; though it says, as a general proposition, that "He who denieth the Father, denieth also the Son; and he who denieth the Son, disbelieveth also the Father." Speaking of ANTI-CHRIST, it merely says, that he who denieth that Jesu is the Meshiha is *An* Antichrist—"A False Meshiha;" that is to say, it would be one of the forms that THE ANTICHRIST would assume.

Of the two readings, that of the Peschito is more in accordance with John's subsequent allusion to the

*Spirit of Antichrist*, than that of Griesbach's text. (See 1 John iv. 2, 3, where he does not identify the denying of Christ with THE ANTICHRIST, but as being of the spirit of THE ANTICHRIST, καὶ τοῦτό ἐστι τὸ τοῦ ἀντιχρίστου). The passage runs thus: " Every spirit that confesseth that Jesus Christ is come in the flesh, is of God: and every spirit that confesseth not that Jesus Christ is come in the flesh, is not of God: and this is that (spirit) of THE ANTICHRIST (τοῦ ἀντιχρίστου), whereof ye have heard it should come ; and even now already is it in the world " (1 John iv. 2, 3). In the Peschito, " Every spirit who confesseth that Jeshu Meshiha hath come in the flesh, is from Aloha. And every spirit who confesseth not that Jeshu hath come in the flesh, is not from Aloha. But this is *from* that False Meshiha, of whom ye have heard that he cometh; and now is in the world already " (" Acts and Epistles," by Etheridge, p. 425.)

I have ventured to direct the attention of the learned to this remarkable variance between the Greek versions of the first Epistle of John and that of the Peschito, because I am not aware that it has hitherto been noticed by any of the numerous controversialists or critical commentators. And yet, if the above renderings of the Peschito be correct, they tend to lessen, if not altogether to obviate, the principal objections to Mr Elliott's views.

Mr Elliott has also, among other things, contended,

with great force of argument, that by ἀντίχριστος, John meant to convey the idea, not of an open, avowed opponent of Christ, but of a pseudo-Christ, one who falsely assumed His power and authority. This interpretation has, however, been objected to as something altogether new, as something arbitrarily invented by the author to suit the purposes of his theory. But on referring to the Peschito, the sense contended for is evidently as ancient as that venerable version. He is there described as a False-Meshiha, the same form of expression as is used when interpreting what in the Greek is called a Pseudo-Christ. " Then if any one shall say unto you, Lo! here is the Meshiha, or there, believe them not. For there shall arise False Meshihas and Prophets of untruth " (Gr. ψευδόχριστοι καὶ ψευδο-προφῆται.) (See Matt. xxiv. 24, and " Syrian Churches," by Etheridge, p. 331.)

Hence the argument assumes the following form:—

In his second Epistle to the Thessalonians, Paul describes some awful power that would thereafter arise, whom he designates as THE MAN OF SIN (ὁ ἄν-θρωπος τῆς ἁμαρτίας), and who, he says, is already, even then, at work in the world, but is prevented from fully developing himself by some let or hindrance. This let or hindrance has, from the earliest times, been understood to refer to the civil authority of the Roman Empire; and the origin of the tradition is

H

traceable to apostolic authority : "Remember ye not, that, when I was yet with you, I told you these things ? And now ye know what withholdeth, that he might be revealed in his time. For the mystery of iniquity doth already work : only he who now letteth will let, till he be taken out of the way" (2 Thess. ii. 5, 6, 7.)

Similarly, John, in his first epistle, makes mention of one whom he calls THE ANTICHRIST (ὁ ἀντί-χριστος), and of whose coming, he says, they had already heard,—"as ye have heard that *Antichrist* shall come,"—apparently alluding to what Paul, by word of mouth, had communicated to the Thessalonians. (See 1 John ii. 18, and following verses.)

There is so striking a similarity between what Paul says of the MAN OF SIN and John's description of ANTICHRIST, that for a long while they have, by many, been looked upon as identical. But of late years the identity has been disputed, not only by Roman Catholics, but also by Protestant writers, who have principally insisted upon two points.

In the first place, they say that the Antichrist of John is one who is to deny the FATHER AND THE SON, that is, who will introduce a system of pure Atheism.

And, secondly, that the definition of the word ANTICHRIST implies an open and avowed opponent of Christ, and is not synonymous with a pseudo-Christ, or false pretender to the authority and power of Christ.

The force of the first of these objections obviously depends upon the purity of the Greek text; and, unfortunately, we have been assured, upon the high authority of Tischendorf, that he has no doubt that, in the very earliest ages after our Holy Scriptures were written, and before the authority of the Church protected them, *wilful alterations, and especially additions*, were made to them. (See Introduction to New Testament, by Tischendorf, xv.) Hence, a question naturally suggests itself, whether the words relied upon in the argument,—viz., "*He is Antichrist that denieth the Father and the Son*,"—be not one of the wilful alterations and additions of an early transcriber?

It cannot but have struck the reader that there is something apparently forced and illogical in the words themselves. They do not sound like genuine, and it is not to be wondered at that commentators are unable to agree as to their meaning. John was not then occupied with the errors of pure Atheism. He was combating the opinions of the GNOSTICS, who fully acknowledged the existence of the Father and also that of the Son, but denied the humanity of the latter. It would, therefore, have been beside the point for John, in his opposition to the Gnostics, to have told his followers that *Antichrist* was he

who denied the FATHER AND THE SON, inasmuch as
the Gnostics would readily have assented to the
proposition, and have been content with repudiating
its applicability to themselves. So that the words,
upon the mere reading of them, suggest a doubt as
to their genuineness, and the doubt thus arising is
almost to a moral certainty confirmed, when, on
turning to the Peschito, we find such remarkable
words omitted from the text of the least corrupted
and the most ancient version in existence.

In some letters I lately published on "The
Apostolic Succession and the Anglican Church,"
I endeavoured to condense the reasons in favour of
the antiquity of the Peschito; but there was one
argument I omitted, and it is a very important one.

In the year 1842, Archdeacon Tatton discovered
some manuscripts in a monastery situated in the
valley of the Natron Lakes; and having brought
them to England, they were deposited in the British
Museum. After remaining there for some time,
they were submitted to the examination of one of the
most learned Syriac scholars of the day, the late Dr
Cureton, who discovered that, among other documents, they contained a copy of some fragments of
the Four Gospels in Syriac. At first he laid them
aside, supposing them to have been a transcript of
the Peschito; but upon a more careful examination,
he arrived at the following important conclusions, in

which all those who are most competent to form an
opinion on such matters are fully agreed:—First,
That the manuscript itself was of the fifth century;
and secondly, That the version of which it was
a transcript was of the second century (Preface,
lxxviii.)

Dr Tregelles does not expressly affirm that in his
opinion the text of the Nitrian Fragments is of the
second century, but he implies it. His words are—
" For while the latter " (the Peschito Gospels) " cannot, in its present state, be deemed an unchanged
production of the SECOND CENTURY, the former " (the
Nitrian Fragments) "bears all the marks of extreme
antiquity " (Smith's " Biblical Dictionary," *tit.* " Version, Syriac," p. 1634).

Now mark the necessary inference, as also bearing
upon the extreme antiquity of the Peschito.

There can, I think, be no doubt but that the
original text of the Peschito has been more or less
tampered with, and yet Dr Cureton, on comparing
it with the Nitrian Fragments, writes as follows:—
" Although there is a marked difference in some
places between the text of the Peschito and that of
these Syriac fragments, the general similarity between
the two is so great as to preclude the possibility of
their having been two altogether distinct and independent versions " (" The Four Gospels in Syriac,"
by the late Dr Cureton, Preface, p. lxvii.)

If this view—and there seems to be no just grounds
to doubt it—be correct, the text of the Peschito, except in so far as there are reasons to suspect its
having been corrupted, is at least as ancient as the
second century. A long and uninterrupted tradition,
corroborated by its internal evidence, assigns to it an
apostolic date! It is, therefore, not without some
show of plausibility that the learned but anonymous
editor of *H KAINH ΔIAΘHKH*, Griesbach's text,
on alluding to the Peschito, expresses himself in the
following terms :—" Of all the ancient versions, the
Syriac is reckoned to be of the highest authority, as
it is supposed to have been written in nearly the
same language as that spoken by Christ and His
disciples " (Introduction, p. xxv.)

The Peschito has also supplied the answer to the
objection arising from the etymology of the word
ANTICHRIST. For it has shown that its authors, who
were probably contemporaries with the apostles, were
not aware of any distinction between an Antichrist
and a Pseudo-Christ, but that they translated them
indifferently by the same word, signifying a False
Meshiha.

I cannot conclude this note without a passing
tribute to the memory of the late Prince Consort, to
whose munificence we are indebted for the publication
of one of the greatest literary treasures we possess—
Dr Cureton's edition of the Nitrian Fragments.

# APPENDIX.

# APPENDIX.

———◆———

*To    *    *    *    *    Professor of Hebrew.*

TEMPLE, E.C.
*January 23, 1869.*

MY DEAR SIR,—You are doubtless aware that, among those who profess to believe in the Christian dispensation, it is universally received that Jesus Christ instituted two ceremonies corresponding to, and in substitution for, the ceremonies of the circumcision and the Passover. We call them respectively " Baptism " and " The Supper of the Lord." It is in regard to the latter, namely, " The Supper of the Lord," that I venture respectfully to solicit your opinion on a point of purely critical interpretation.

Amongst our sacred records there are four accounts of what fell from Christ on the occasion of His instituting this ceremony—one by Matthew, another by Mark, a third by Luke, and a fourth by Paul. Each of these

several accounts are held in equal esteem and veneration
by Christians.   But they are not *verbatim* the same.   In
Matthew and Mark, it is recorded that Christ, being assembled on the occasion of the Passover with His apostles,
" took bread and blessed" (or gave thanks), " and break,
and gave to His disciples (in Mark, to them, αὐτοῖς),
"and said, 'Take, eat; this is my body;'" in Greek,
τοῦτό ἐστι τὸ σῶμά μου.   (See Matt. xxvi. 26, and Mark
xiv. 22.)  Luke and Paul substantially agree with Matthew
and Mark, but they supplement these important words,
" Which is given " (Paul, " broken ") " for you."   So that,
according to them, the words were, " Take, eat; this is my
body, which is given" (or broken) "for you."   According
to Luke and Paul, Christ further added, " This do in remembrance of me."   (See Luke xxii. 19; Paul, 1 Cor.
xi. 24.)

   You are probably aware that a difference of opinion has
long prevailed among Christians as to the true interpretation to be put upon these words.   On the part of the
Roman Catholics, and also of the members of the Greek
Church since 1672, it is said that the language should be
construed according to the literal signification of the
words ; that they admit of no other interpretation ; and
that, when so construed, they conclusively prove that the
sacramental bread is the actual material body of the Lord
Jesus Christ.   On the other hand, it is by Protestants
maintained that Christ did not mean to convey that the

bread He held in His hand was really Himself, or that its
nature as bread had undergone any change; but that,
intending to institute a ceremony commemorative of His
death, which was then about to take place, He selected
bread as symbolic of Himself, as something His followers
were thereafter to partake of in remembrance of Him: and
that the words, "This is my body," or "This is my body
which is given" (or broken) "for you," are not necessarily
to be construed literally, any more than a similar form of
expression often adopted by Him, such as, "I *am* the
door," "I *am* the good shepherd," not meaning that He
was in fact either a door or a shepherd, but that a door
and a shepherd spiritually represented Him.

The controversy has continued among Christians during
a period of many centuries, each party relying upon the
*Greek text*, and each contenting himself with his own interpretation of it. But no new light was thrown upon the
subject till very lately, when it occurred to the late Dr
Adam Clarke to question the propriety of the words imputed to Christ. For he contended that Christ spoke in
Chaldee or Chaldeo-Syriac, and not in Greek, and that the
words which in the Greek are rendered by "τοῦτό ἐστι
τὸ σῶμά μου," and in English by "This is my body," are,
in the Syriac version, "honau pagreé," and that this form
of expression might with equal accuracy be translated in
either way, "This *is* my body," or "This *represents* my
body."

You will observe, that so far as the controversy between the Protestants and Roman Catholics is concerned, it was not necessary for Dr Adam Clarke to have gone beyond what I have above stated, viz., that, consistently with the idiom of the Chaldeo-Syriac, the form of expression, "honau pagreé," was equally capable of either interpretation. But that learned theologian went a step further, and said that in the Hebrew or Chaldeo-Syriac there was no word to express "*to represent*," and that if Christ meant to say, "this *represents* my body," He could have done so in no other way than by using words which also meant "this *is* my body."

I am not aware that any one controverted the soundness of the views suggested by Dr Adam Clarke till the subject was taken up by the late equally learned Cardinal Wiseman, who, in some lectures he delivered at St Mary's, Moorfields, during the Lent of 1863, and which he afterwards published, on "The Principal Doctrines and Practices of the Catholic Church," declared that the assertions of Dr Adam Clarke were most incorrect, and that the Syriac has plenty of words, more than any European language, for the purpose required, namely, to express "to represent," "to denote," "to signify," and "to typify;" whilst, at the same time, he agreed with Dr Adam Clarke in that the Syriac was the language spoken by our Saviour, as you will perceive on referring to Lecture xiv., p. 150, of the accompanying volume.

Hence it is that these two distinguished authors, both of them men of great learning, and, we are bound to assume, of equal integrity, are directly at issue upon a point of construction depending upon the critically correct interpretation of a language in respect to which their readers, for the most part, are in the profoundest ignorance. Under these circumstances, it has occurred to me to solicit your aid and assistance. Your authority on such a subject is held in equal, if not in higher, esteem than that of either disputant; and your impartiality can admit of no question, inasmuch as you are no doubt equally indifferent to either of their respective views.

I take the liberty of forwarding a copy of the Lectures, lest I should be suspected of misrepresenting the argument, and refer you to vol. ii., p. 190.

Should you kindly consent to favour me with an answer, I would further venture to trespass upon your indulgence, by requesting you also to refer to the several texts mentioned by Cardinal Wiseman, commencing at the last paragraph, p. 179, and concluding with, " Fourthly, Exodus xii. 11. ' This *is* the Lord's Passover.' " In point of fact, in all these several passages, is the verb " *to be* " expressly mentioned, or are they all, and if not all, how many of them, expressed by a similar form of speech to that of " honau pagre6," which we translate by " This *is* my body ? "

Your opinion, therefore, is respectfully requested upon

the two following points :—First, On comparing the views
of Dr Adam Clarke and Cardinal Wiseman, how far, in
your opinion, is the one or the other borne out by the
idiom of the Chaldeo-Syriac language? Secondly, Is the
form of expression, in the several texts referred to,
similar to the form of expression used by Christ in
instituting the Lord's Supper?

Believe me, my dear Sir, yours very truly,

F. D. MASSY DAWSON.

---

*To* F. D. MASSY DAWSON, *Esq.*

1. MY DEAR SIR,—I do not consider myself called upon
to examine the theological propositions postulated in the
paper of questions submitted to me, as agreed to by all
Christian sects, viz. :—

a. That the Founder of the Christian religion abolished
circumcision ;

b. That He instituted baptism in its stead ;

c. That He abolished the Jewish Passover ;

d. That He instituted the " Lord's Supper " instead
of the Jewish Passover.

2. I address myself to the examination of the words, "This is my body," which occur in the account of the institution of the "Lord's Supper," in order to ascertain, by the usual rules of grammatical interpretation,—1st, Whether these words *must* or *may* be taken in a literal sense; or else, 2d, Whether these words *must* or *may* be taken in a figurative sense.

Whatever result will be legitimately arrived at with respect to the words, "This is my body," will naturally apply with equal right to the words, "This is my blood," which likewise occur in the institution of the "Lord's Supper."

3. The formula, "This is my body," occurs in the New Testament four times with reference to the "Lord's Supper," viz. :—

In the Gospel of St Matthew xxvi. 26 ;

,, ,, St Mark xiv. 22 ;

,, ,, St Luke xxii. 19 ;

In the 1st Epistle to the Corinthians, xi. 24 ;

without any variation of style, viz., τοῦτό ἐστι τὸ σῶμά μου ; except that in the Epistle the word μου is placed immediately after τοῦτο.

4. As it may, with a high degree of probability, be assumed that Jesus, in His intercourse with His disciples (and the people generally), made use of the idiom then current in Palestine, and especially in Galilee, the native province of

the majority of His first followers,—viz., the Aramaic, that is, the so-called Chaldee of Palestine, such as we have it in the Jewish Targumim or versions of the Scriptures, and which borders very closely on the Syriac as used by the Christian Syrians, whose literature we still possess,—it is considered important to know how the Syriac version of the New Testament renders the formula, " τοῦτό ἐστι τὸ σῶμά μου."

5. In the Syriac versions the sacramental formula does not exhibit that perfect identity of diction which exists in the four texts of the Greek original. For while Matthew, Luke, and the Epistle to the Corinthians present the same reading, viz., "hunau pagri" (the vowels are to be read according to the Italian or German manner of pronunciation), literally, " This is my body "—the personal pronoun being in the Semitic languages the substitute for the copula "is"—there is, in the Syriac Gospel of St Mark an additional word, viz., "ithau*h*i" (the italic letter is mute), which expresses "being." The words are, " Hunu ithau*h*i pagri," which cannot be translated otherwise than "This is my body." The first word, " hunu," "this," differs from the first Syriac word in the other texts, inasmuch as these have " hunau," a compound of the demonstrative " this" and the personal pronoun " he or it," which is the substitute for the copula. As this personal pronoun is wanting in the composition of the first word in the text of

St Mark, the substitute for the copula is supplied by the subsequent word, " ithau*h*i." This word is not, however, like the English or the Greek copula, the third person singular of the verb "to be;" it is a word which admits of no variation (ith = to the Hebrew שֵׁי_ "Yesh," and to the Arabic ايس "Ais "), and to which are added the pronominal suffixes usually added to a substantive in the plural. If it were required to render the translation of such a form intelligible to a reader unacquainted with Semitic languages, the translation would literally be, " existences of him or it;" but the signification would necessarily be—"he or it is." In fine, the Syriac version, in all the four texts referred to, yields a full equivalent for the English formula, "This is my body."

6. In the Semitic languages the present tense of the verb "to be," which, in Arian languages, forms the copula between the subject and the predicate of a proposition, *cannot* appear, because the Semitic languages have not what we call the present tense of a verb. When it is required to express *present action*, the active participle of the verb is employed and the copula is, in this case too, mentally supplied. Instead of the copula, a personal pronoun, masculine or feminine, in the singular or in the plural, as the subject may require, is inserted; but it may be omitted without endangering the clearness of the proposition. Thus, if I wish to say in Hebrew, *e.g.*, "Thy

I

brother stands before thee," I use words which literally mean, "Thy brother he standing before thee," or, with equal propriety, "Thy brother standing before thee,"—the copula would, by an Arian, be in each case mentally supplied before the word "standing."

The past and the future tenses of the verb "to be" are in frequent use, as, *e.g.*, the 2d verse of the first chapter in Genesis shows : " And the earth *was* without form and void;" in Hebrew, " Wehaarets *hayethah* thohoo wavohu."

7. From the grammatical form, by itself, of the formula. " This is my body," as expressed in Syriac or in any other Semitic idiom, it is impossible to determine whether the words have a literal or a figurative meaning. That propositions precisely similar in form have frequently a literal meaning, everybody admits.

8. That this form is *also* susceptible of a figurative interpretation can be proved by numerous scriptural instances.

Independently of the texts adduced for this purpose by Adam Clarke in "A Discourse on the Nature and Design of the Eucharist," p. 51 (some of which are irrelevant to this question), which are discussed by Wiseman in the fifteenth Lecture, p. 179, *et seq.*, and in all of which the copula is omitted, I will quote, by way of illustration, Exodus iv. 22, where the Lord says, " Israel (is) my first-born ;" and Jeremiah xxxi. 9, where the Lord says, " But Ephraim he (is) my first-born." In both instances the predicate, "first-born," must be, and universally is, interpreted *figuratively*. In the *literal* sense, the two texts would contradict each other. Wiseman, while insisting on the literal sense of "This *is* my body," admits that, when the *subject treated in a text* allows a figurative mode of speech, the *form* of the words, in the same arrangement, offers no obstacle to a figurative interpretation (Lect. xv., p. 187).

A figurative sense may be given, according to Wiseman, to the terms employed in "the *explanation of some symbol*, such as the interpretation of a vision, a parable, or a prophecy" (p. 186).

9. Admitting, for a moment, the hermeneutical rule set up by Wiseman, I may still allow a Protestant to argue with (what seems to me) consistency thus: "Christ prescribed to His followers the performance, in remembrance of His passion, of a symbolical act, saying, *Take ! eat !* He then *explained* the signification of this *symbolical act*, saying, This (act) is (in remembrance of, or any words to the same effect) my body (broken), &c. Indeed there are other expressions *necessarily* figurative in the sequel, the *immediate* sequel to these words. For Christ proceeds to say : 'I will drink no more of the fruit of the vine until that day that I drink it new in the kingdom of God' (Mark xiv. 25). All this is surely figurative! Again, St Luke and St Paul, who must undoubtedly have com-

prehended quite as well as a modern scholar the terms used by Christ on that occasion, make Christ say, 'This cup is the New Testament,' &c. (St Luke xxii. 20, and 1 Cor. xi. 25.) Now this phrase has a metaphor in its composition. A *cup* is *not* a *testament*, except in a figurative sense." Wiseman himself is aware of the impropriety of connecting the word "*this*" τοῦτο, with "bread" (p. 212), and his manner of reconciling his literal interpretation with that admitted impropriety does not seem to me felicitous. (See Lect. xvi., p. 212, from "In the first place"—"essentially.") Consequently, *if* Wiseman's hermeneutical rule be valid, the instituting words of the Eucharist bear with perfect propriety a figurative meaning.

10. The argument quoted by Wiseman (Lect. xv., p. 196, and "Horæ Syriacæ," p. 59) from Eastern believers in the real presence is not conclusive. St Maruthas Tangritensis, in the fourth century, argues that the faithful receive really the body and the blood of Jesus, "because Christ did not call it type and image, but verily this is my body and this is my blood." Now, if Bishop St Maruthas wished his hearers and readers to believe that the expression *verily* was a part of the New Testament text, he deserved of course no credit : but if the word *verily* is nothing but the Bishop's comment, the argument may be fairly turned against him by any Protestant, thus :

" If Christ had intended to use, in a *literal* sense, words
which every ordinary hearer could not but understand
*figuratively*, he would have added such explanatory terms
as the unexpected meaning of his words rendered necessary ; but Christ did *not* add such explanatory terms ;
*ergo*, He meant His words to be understood as they certainly must have been understood by His hearers, that
is, in a *figurative* sense."

11. I go further, and say, that Wiseman's hermeneutical
canon is *not* borne out by scriptural practice. It does *not*
appear, as Wiseman maintains, that figurative terms are,
in Scripture, limited to texts which treat of the interpretation of " a vision, or a parable, or a prophecy." There
cannot exist a more matter-of-fact subject than a legal
enactment. There is, in such a subject, nothing at all re-
sembling " a vision, or a parable, or a prophecy." Still, in
the law respecting the severe chastisement of a slave by
his master (Exod. xxi. 21), it is decided that, if the slave
do not immediately die under the master's hand, the master is not to be punished ; for, adds the text, the slave is
the silver of the master—כִּי כַסְפּוֹ הוּא " for he (is) his
silver." A slave is *not* silver. The expression has a *figurative* import, viz., "the slave is (a property purchased by)
the silver of the master." If, then, a metaphorical sense
*may*, and occasionally *must*, be put on words occurring in
*any* kind of scriptural texts, it follows that a figurative

expression must be admissible in the words "This is my body," in a text which is, moreover, connected with propositions (see above) plainly used metaphorically.

12. Adam Clarke was decidedly wrong in stating that the Syriac (or the Semitic languages in general) possesses no terms wherewith to express "to mean," "to signify," "to denote," &c. ("Discourse," &c., p. 51). The fact is (as Wiseman has shown in his instructive work "Horæ Syriacæ," p. 18–56) that Jesus might very well, had He chosen, have said in Aramaic (or Hebrew), "This is *like*, or *as*, or *the representative of*, or *the figure of*, or *the symbol of*, &c., my body." Not that the intention of using "This is my body" in a figurative sense would have rendered such a periphrasis *necessary;* but the genius of the Semitic languages would not have stood in the way of such an amplification. I cannot account for the learned Adam Clarke's error on this head. Every tyro in biblical studies ought to know that the words for "image" and "likeness or similitude" occur in the 26th verse of the very first chapter of Genesis (Hebrew עֶלֶם and דְּמוּת; Aramaic the same; Arabic صورة and مشال). It is surprising that this text escaped Adam Clarke's attention; and equally surprising that Wiseman, so far as I remember, forgot to urge this proof against Adam Clarke.

13. Whether there be *other* texts in the New Testament

which enforce or not the literal sense of the formula, "This is my body," &c., is no part of the question submitted to me. I therefore refrain from pushing my investigation beyond the limits set by the inquirer.

Believe me, dear Sir, yours truly,

\*   \*   \*   \*

THE END.

## By the same Author.

———◆———

## THE APOSTOLIC SUCCESSION OF THE ANGLICAN CHURCH.

Crown 8vo, 1s., sewed.

———————

## THOUGHTS ON THE MILLENNIUM AND FIRST RESURRECTION.

Crown 8vo, 1s., sewed.

www.ingramcontent.com/pod-product-compliance
Lightning Source LLC
Chambersburg PA
CBHW020236030726
47497CB00009B/3121